CONCEAL: LINCOLN

EAGLE TACTICAL BOOK THREE

WILLOW FOX

SLOWBURN
PUBLISHING

Conceal: Lincoln

Eagle Tactical Book THREE

Willow Fox

Published by Slow Burn Publishing

CHAPTER ONE

LINCOLN

Exhaustion didn't even begin to explain the weariness behind my gaze.

I stumbled into the town coffee shop.

The bell jingled on the door as I entered, and the aroma of coffee beans gave me my first fix of the morning like a drug.

I needed more.

"Next," the girl behind the counter snapped.

Without my morning cup of coffee yet, I hadn't had the jolt to wake me. I stammered forward up to the counter. "Hey, Skylar."

Since when did she work here? Last I heard, she came to visit her older brother in town.

Apparently, she wasn't leaving anytime soon.

"What can I get for you?" she asked.

She stood behind the counter wearing a brown apron and matching hat.

While I felt fatigued, her eyes softened, and the corners of her lips quirked up when she seemed to recognize me.

"Hey, Lincoln, right?"

"Yes," I said as my gaze glanced over the chalkboard behind her with the list of available drinks and specials.

The owner always liked to change it up, and there was never a plain black coffee on the menu.

"What do you recommend?" Making a decision took too much effort at this hour.

"Brewing your coffee at home," Skylar said. "The coffee here is way overpriced but don't tell my boss I said that, or I'll get fired."

I snorted under my breath. "Noted. I'll have whatever's strong and make it black."

I couldn't deal with sugar at this early hour.

The sun hadn't even come up yet, and while I should have been in bed, I still had another hour until I usually woke up.

I hadn't been able to sleep, and with the recent shooting at the restaurant, my coffee maker had been toast.

Sleep had eluded me, even on a Sunday morning when I should have been able to relax and take the day off.

Stress didn't typically bother me, but after two mobsters had gunned down the restaurant, I was on high alert, ready on a whim. It resulted from my time in the military that forced me to be up at a moment's notice.

Skylar tapped away at the register before I shoved my credit card into the chip reader to pay.

A blonde stepped forward with giant sunglasses on, the kind a woman wears to either hide a black eye or to try to conceal her identity. Both of those seemed plausible.

"Excuse me," she said. "I ordered a coffee ten minutes ago."

"It's been five," Skylar said, "and your drink is on the counter waiting for you to pick it up."

"You didn't call my name," the woman wearing sunglasses said.

"Heather."

"It's Harper," she said, correcting Skylar.

Skylar stepped to the side where the drink sat perched on the counter, waiting to be picked up. "Same difference. Do you want your coffee or not?"

Another barista worked on my drink while Harper stood, arms folded across her chest.

"You need to make me another latte," Harper said. She unfolded her arms long enough to slide her sunglasses back up as they began to slip down her face.

"I don't need to do anything, ma'am," Skylar said. She turned and faced the register. "Next!"

The barista preparing my coffee headed over with the piping hot liquid and secured a lid to the cup. "Lincoln."

Harper snatched the coffee before I could get my hands on it. "I'm going to be late."

She stole my drink and stormed out of the shop, hurrying to her car.

"I hope she likes it black," I muttered under my breath—what a perfect way to start my morning.

I should have stayed in bed.

———

I picked up lunch and drove over to Mason's house to check up on him. It'd been a few weeks since he'd been shot by the mafia protecting his high school sweetheart, Hazel Agron.

Arriving at his house, before I could even lift my hand to the door, Hazel pounced. She was faster than their dog, Bear, that they'd adopted after Mason's uncle passed.

Hazel yanked open the door and threw her arms around me. "Thank you for coming," she whispered into my ear.

"Of course. I brought lunch," I said and lifted the bag of Chinese food takeout to show what I'd fetched.

Hazel ushered me inside Mason's house and shut the door.

I handed over the bag of food while I shucked off my coat and boots.

"Smells good," Mason said with a grunt as he pushed himself up from the sofa. "What'd you bring?"

"Orange Beef, Sesame Chicken, Sweet and Sour Shrimp, Mongolia Beef, and a few appetizers. I wasn't sure what everyone wanted, so I tried to get a variety," I said.

I hadn't wanted to come empty-handed, and Hazel had been busy looking after Mason. She deserved a meal she didn't have to cook.

"I'm famished," Mason said.

He sluggishly ambled toward the table, the injury of two bullets getting the better of him.

"How are the restaurant repairs coming?" Mason asked.

Hazel unveiled the contents of the brown paper bag with all the dishes while I rummaged through the drawers for silverware. There were already paper plates on the table and chopsticks along with plasticware for eating.

"Slow and practically non-existent," I said. "Can I get you something to drink?"

I'd visited Mason over the years enough to have memorized not only the layout, but also where he kept everything in the cabinets.

"Water is good."

I grabbed three glasses from the cabinet and filled each of them with water. "How have you been feeling?" I asked, turning to face Mason but still keeping an eye on the glass so that I didn't make a mess.

"Tired, sore, I feel like I've been shot, twice." Mason laughed and sat down with a gruffness that I hadn't seen cross his face in the past.

He winced, trying to hide his obvious discomfort. "I'm feeling better already and anxious to get back to business."

"Ready to kick me out of Eagle Tactical?" I asked, mildly joking with him. Jaxson, one of our other special force's brothers, kept insisting I join the guys. We were all military brothers and had served together.

On occasion, I had helped them out when they needed an extra set of hands for a case or an assignment in the field.

"No, you're staying. I just want to get back in the field with you again."

The truth was that I loved the restaurant that I'd worked hard to make a success, but getting back to work there would still be a few months.

The restaurant needed a lot of repairs. The dining room had been trashed by the dozens of bullets that had rained down on the interior. I had an insurance agent working with me for the repairs, but it would take time.

I brought two glasses of water to the table for Hazel and Mason. I filled the third glass and set that down in front of my plate, taking a seat at the kitchen table.

"You look like you're doing better," I said. Being shot took time to heal, physical therapy to get a range of motion back, among other things.

Hazel remained quiet as she dished out her lunch on the plate in front of her.

Mason grunted. "I'm ready to get out of this house. No offense to Hazel," he said and glanced at her. "You've done a wonderful job taking care of me. I'm just not used to having someone look after me."

Hazel smiled and patted his good arm. "No offense taken, and I understand. I'd love to go out and get a drink, socialize."

He'd always been independent, even with the ladies. I couldn't remember Mason ever having a girlfriend live with him. He'd kept his relationships pretty quiet, though I'd seen him take a woman home once or twice from the bar.

"We should do that tonight," Mason said.

"You're not supposed to be drinking," Hazel reminded him.

He grumbled under his breath.

"She's right," I said, stepping in to defend Hazel. "We all just want what's best for you. If you're on painkillers, you can't be drinking."

I took a sip of water and placed the glass back on the wooden table. "If you want to come out tonight for an hour, just to get out of the house, I can drive you home."

The bar wasn't that far from Mason's place. It was too long a distance for him to walk after his injuries, but it wouldn't take long for me to drop him off if he wanted to see the guys for an hour.

Anything longer, and I worried that he'd overdo it and tax himself. Mason wasn't good at asking for help.

Mason took a bite of lunch, his gaze on the food in front of him.

I couldn't tell if he was pleased with my suggestion or was going to ask me to leave.

"An hour's better than nothing."

"How about we all meet after dinner but a little on the early side?" Hazel asked. "That way, the bar won't be as crowded."

Her gaze met mine, and she didn't have to say the real reason she wanted to meet earlier.

I sensed it already.

Mason would be too exhausted later in the evening.

He had dark circles under his eyes. His hair was messy, but that was probably more because he hadn't showered today.

"That sounds good, and I'm sure the others will be on board with that too. I'll text them and let them know to meet us at the bar at seven tonight," I said.

I finished the last of my lunch.

Mason looked beat, and I didn't want him to feel that he had to entertain me or be kept awake.

"Take a nap. I'll see you tonight," I said. I helped Hazel put the rest of the food away and into the fridge.

Mason disappeared down the hall and into his room to rest.

"How have you been doing?" I asked, keeping my voice low.

I didn't want to disturb Mason or have him overhear our conversation.

"It's been a lot," Hazel said, her eyes trained on the kitchen table as she tossed the dirty paper plates into the trash bin.

I grabbed the few pieces of silverware and glasses and took the items to the sink to clean.

I didn't want to leave a mess for her to deal with. She already had enough to do to take care of Mason.

"He appreciates your help and you being here, whether he tells it to you or not," I said.

"I know," Hazel said. She wiped down the table.

Standing in front of the sink, I waited for the tap water to run hot before I filled up the sink to wash the dishes from lunch and quite a few in the sink that had been left from breakfast.

"You don't have to do the dishes."

"I know," I said. I didn't budge from in front of the sink. Once the water grew warm, I plugged the drain and let the empty side of the sink fill with water.

Hazel pointed under the sink. "Dish soap is down there."

"Thanks." I already knew where Mason kept the soap. I opened the cabinet and retrieved the liquid. I squeezed a few drops into the sink. Suds formed as water poured in and made bubbles. "How are things between you and Mason?"

"Fine." Hazel's eyes widened as she glanced up at me. "Why? Did he say something?"

Her brow furrowed, and she shuffled her feet while she stood in the kitchen and seemed uncomfortable with my question.

I hadn't meant to offend her or cause any drama between the two of them. "No, I just know that moving to a new city can be challenging, and the fact you don't know anyone and are stuck taking care of Mason, it's probably a lot to deal with on your own."

"What are you, a psychologist?" Hazel asked. She folded her arms across her chest.

"No, I'm just used to being an ear for a lot of the guys. Mason used to talk about you a lot."

Maybe I shouldn't have said anything, but I found it hard to ignore the obvious fact that they both liked each other a lot.

At least I knew Mason liked Hazel. I didn't want to see her push him away when he eventually could take care of himself again.

"He did?" Her voice caught in her throat. "About what?" She leaned against the kitchen counter, her gaze on me the entire time as I washed the dishes by hand.

"He always compared the girls he dated to you. He'd talk about how he was young and stupid and had let you go away to school."

"I never went to college."

"Oh." I didn't know what to say to that.

She was the girl he'd gone to boarding school with and compared every girl after to. While most of the guys hadn't talked as openly about their pasts, Mason had regretted letting her go.

"I was supposed to," Hazel said, "but it's a long story, and I'd rather change the subject."

"Sure."

"Mason's a good guy. It's just a lot right now, taking care of him and trying to make him comfortable. I won't even tell you how difficult it is to get him into the shower."

I chuckled under my breath. "Mason's a big guy." He was twice the size of Hazel. "You're not asking me to bathe him, are you?"

Hazel grinned. "Would you?"

"No." I assumed she'd been joking, but I wasn't taking any chances.

There were some lines we didn't cross.

She scrunched her nose and laughed. "Damn. It was worth a shot."

I finished the last of the dishes and left them on the drying rack, stacked to the brim. "Anything else you need help with around here? Other than bathing your boyfriend."

Hazel shook her head. "I've got it. I'll tidy up the place while Mason's napping. I am looking forward to going out tonight. Don't hold it against me if I get wasted."

"As long as you don't drive home."

Her eyes shined with a glint of happiness, something that I hadn't seen the entire time that I'd been over during lunch.

The thought of getting out and socializing seemed to have shifted her mood for the better. Hopefully, it would help Mason too.

————

I arrived early at the bar to make sure that I could grab a comfortable booth for all of us to sit together.

In the corner of the bar, there was a booth that would easily seat our crew.

I claimed it before anyone else could, and while I wanted a beer, I'd wait to step up to the bar until one of the other guys came and could watch our table.

"Jaxson!" I waved to him as he shuffled into the bar, glancing around for the rest of us.

"Where's Ariella?" I asked as he scooted into the booth seat across from me.

His eyes narrowed.

"What? It's just the two of us." I already knew they were sleeping together, but the rest of the office wasn't supposed to know.

He was her boss.

Technically, the entire Eagle Tactical team was Ariella's boss, but Jaxson was sleeping with her.

They were also living together, but that wasn't because they were involved. It had been a result of her house burning down months ago.

"I don't know. Ariella will be here soon." Jaxson rested his hands on the wood table. "We thought it'd be a good idea to show up separate."

"Everything okay in paradise?"

I hadn't noticed any drama, but they were good at hiding their relationship.

Which was ironic, since Jaxson had been testy and short-tempered for the brief time they'd worked together before they'd fallen into bed.

She made him happy, and if the other guys couldn't see it, they were blind.

Jaxson nodded toward the door where Declan came through, along with Mason and Hazel trailing behind.

I scooted out of the booth. "I'll get us drinks," I said.

Already, the bar had grown crowded, and patrons waited for their drinks. I leaned against the bar, my hands clasped together, awaiting my turn.

A soft voice cleared her throat beside me as she hurried up to the bar and perched herself on the empty stool.

The coffee thief.

I gestured the bartender over to me next, but he hadn't come and taken my drink order yet.

"You," I said, landing my gaze on the girl who had snatched my hot coffee and left me grumpy earlier that morning.

She laughed under her breath and avoided my stare. Her long hair covered part of her face, hiding from me.

Was it on purpose?

The bartender headed over to me. "What can I get for you?" he asked.

"Let me buy you a drink," Harper said, and she shifted on the barstool to face me.

I wanted to push the long strand of hair out of her eyes and behind her ear, but I kept my hands to myself. "I'll have a beer," I said to the bartender. "Whatever's on tap."

While I had come up to the bar to order drinks for the table, I found myself interested in the mysterious new girl who had shown up in Breckenridge.

Was she here on vacation like everyone else who didn't live in the small town?

Harper retrieved her credit card from her wallet and slid it across the bar's counter to the bartender. "It's on me. I'll have a screwdriver."

The bartender poured my beer first and then went to work on making Harper a screwdriver.

While I wasn't one to let a woman pay for my drinks or buy me dinner, Harper had gotten under my skin earlier that morning.

The least she could do was apologize, and since that wasn't happening, I'd settle with a beer on tap.

"Thank you," I said to her, sipping my beer. The barstool beside Harper was empty.

I glanced back at my friends. They were giving me a thumb's up gesture when they noticed I spoke with Harper.

"It's the least I can do after this morning," Harper said. "I'm dangerous before I've had my coffee."

I sat on the stool and shifted around to face her. "You and me both."

She wasn't the only one who dealt in danger, but I held my tongue.

She didn't need to know about my life, who I was, or what I did for a living. I liked the mysterious factor for once.

Harper knew nothing about me, and I could keep it that way.

The bartender handed Harper her screwdriver, and she sipped the orange liquid, her eyes wincing with each taste.

Was she not used to the drink being strong? She had ordered vodka and orange juice.

"What are you doing in Breckenridge?" I asked.

Most tourists came in winter to the resort for skiing and snowboarding. We attracted watersports like rafting and kayaking in the summer, but spring typically was quiet and calm with newcomers.

"I'm here to blow up the town."

CHAPTER TWO

HARPER

I'd seen him enter the bar, the handsome man whose coffee I'd swiped earlier that morning at the coffee shop.

I couldn't help the anger that sizzled through my veins while I waited for my caffeine fix.

It hadn't been bad enough that the girl behind the register had been rude and overcharged me, she had also gotten my name wrong.

Then he'd strode in and smiled at her. One look, and she was putty to him.

Were they a couple?

Gross.

I wanted to puke. I also wanted my coffee really bad.

The barista was already preparing whatever the hell concoction he ordered, but mine was nowhere to be seen, and they hadn't called my name to tell me it was ready.

I'd been a spoiled brat and snatched his hot coffee. I'd done it dozens of times on the studio set, but this wasn't a movie studio. I'd been stupid and rude.

And the coffee was awful. Bitter and black. I deserved it.

I'd spent the day in my motel room.

I hadn't rented a place at the resort where I'd read the accommodations had been far more luxurious.

My agent set me up at the shithole so no one would recognize me.

It sucked.

My day had gone from bad that morning with no coffee, to worse when I discovered that the studio executives had opted to hire a private security team to keep me out of trouble.

I liked trouble.

At least that's what the studio and the tabloids wrote.

I'd made a reputation for myself as *The Vixen*. It hadn't been hard, and my agent had told me that no publicity was bad publicity.

Was that true?

It had landed me quite a few new movie roles, and I'd been mentioned on all the entertainment shows and magazines on a semi-regular basis.

I was the girl your mother warned you about. The one who stole your boyfriend and slept with a man just to toy with him.

Except that wasn't the real me.

I could still count the number of men I'd slept with in my lifetime on one hand.

I was shy, introverted, and hated being alone.

The rest was an act. It was a good thing I was an actress and a damned good one.

I'd had the world fooled, and somewhere along the way I'd fooled myself into believing I'd been happy.

I sat at a lonely table, nursing a vodka and orange juice—a screwdriver.

I wanted to appear tough. I couldn't drink anything girly, even though it's what I'd have preferred.

At any moment, someone could recognize me and snap a picture of Harper Madison. It would be on all of social media in a matter of minutes. I had to tread carefully.

When I saw *him* stalk into the bar with a purpose, he strode over and sat down at the booth in the corner, the largest booth there was.

I couldn't help but stare at him, transfixed.

I wanted to go over, strike up a conversation and apologize for being a brat earlier, but I couldn't move from my position.

His name was Lincoln. At least that had been the name on his coffee cup unless the girl had gotten his name wrong too?

His friends showed up, and eventually, he headed to the bar for a drink. That was my excuse, my chance to talk to him, which led me to a bad joke and the concern that he might have me arrested.

He'd been polite, and I'd earned his attention after buying him a beer. It was the least I could do, and while I should have come out and apologized for my behavior that morning, I found it too difficult to voice the words.

"What are you doing in Breckenridge?" he asked.

"I'm here to blow up the town." It was a joke. A lame joke since I'd shown up to help film a movie.

"Excuse me?" Lincoln asked, his eyes wide and mouth agape.

My joke about being here to blow up the town hadn't gone over well.

He put his drink down hard on the bar, forceful.

"It was a joke."

He grabbed my wrist and pulled me off the stool. His eyes raked over my body, sending a shiver down my spine.

Did he recognize me?

I hadn't been in disguise, but the bar was dimly lit, and this was a small town.

"Do I need to call the sheriff?" Lincoln asked. His grip didn't loosen from my wrist.

Quickly, he could yank both of my arms behind my back and restrain me.

Is that what he wanted to do?

A small part of me wanted that from him, his dominance.

He was a good-looking guy, and his brooding nature sent a shiver down my spine and made me feel warm and tingly all over.

"It was a joke," I repeated and shrugged my arm in an attempt to unclasp myself from his clutches. "Would you let me go?"

His eyes were tight and narrow, his jaw sharp. Is this what it was like to piss him off?

I didn't want to witness his wrath when he was angry.

"There's nothing funny about threatening our town," Lincoln said.

He unlatched his hand from my wrist, and I pulled my arm away in a hurry. I rubbed my wrist where his hand had held me tight, but there was no mark.

"Why are you really here, Harper? Is that even your real name?"

I exhaled a heavy breath through my nose, staring at my wrist, surprised there wasn't a bruise, a red mark, any evidence that he'd touched me. "Yes. No." I could still feel his firm grip, even though his hands were nowhere near my body.

"Which is it?"

"It's complicated," I said.

Harper was my stage name, the name that everyone knew me by, but it wasn't the name I was given at birth. I didn't have many friends, and the few people who knew me called me Harper because they'd only come to know me after I'd made a name for myself. Except for the few people like my agent and the studio executives who called me whatever they wanted whenever they wanted.

His eyes softened. "What do you want me to call you?" he asked. His words were calm, soft, and his tone seemed genuine, like he cared about me.

Didn't he recognize me as Harper Madison?

Maybe he didn't watch chick flicks. Perhaps he'd never seen me before this morning in the coffee shop.

"Harper is fine." I couldn't hide who I was, even if I wanted to try.

A part of me wanted to hide, escape, and let no one know about my past.

Filming in a small town had its advantages, but living there, I wasn't sure I was cut out for it.

I was pretty sure I wasn't ready to settle down in a town with less than a thousand people. The studio where we filmed in Los Angeles had more people working on a set than the town of Breckenridge.

"You're Lincoln, right?" I asked.

His lips quirked upwards with a faint smile. "Yes, I am." He sipped his beer.

"Can we do this again, start over?" I asked and held out my hand to introduce myself. "I'm Harper."

"Lincoln," he said and shook my hand with a laugh. He tilted his head slightly to the side, staring at me. "You never did answer why you're in town."

"Oh, right." I laughed under my breath. I guess I wasn't getting out of it that easily. "I'm here filming something small for the studio."

It was a little white lie.

While I was here to film a movie for the studio, it wasn't small or insignificant. The budget alone was probably more than the town's worth.

Lincoln finished his beer and gestured the bartender over for a second.

Against my better judgment, I ordered a second screwdriver.

The drinks were strong, but I didn't want the night to end. It was still early, and the handsome stranger, Lincoln, I'd won his full, undivided attention, and it wasn't because of my celebrity status.

"I'll have another one too," I said.

Lincoln pulled out his credit card. "They're on me," he said to the bartender, handing over his credit card. "Start a tab."

"Are you here filming a commercial or something?" Lincoln asked. His fingers drummed against the bar counter as he sat facing me.

Our knees brushed against each other, and my body tingled at the thought of what he looked like undressed. "Something like that," I said.

Lincoln was albeit handsome but not my usual type. He was strong, muscular, and looked quite a bit like a lumberjack with his thick beard and outdoorsy attire.

I'd never met a lumberjack before.

The bartender brought us both our drinks and placed them on the counter.

Leaning in, I reached for my drink at the same time Lincoln did, breathing in his masculine scent.

I momentarily closed my eyes as the bar felt several degrees warmer.

Was my face flushed?

Could he sense my attraction? I barely knew him.

What had gotten into me?

I didn't drink that often because I was a feather when it came to alcohol.

No doubt I could easily get knocked on my ass, but that was the result of watching everything I ate for filming. My agent had been strict and in-my-face, reminding me to count calories because the camera was unapologetic.

Sipping my drink, I avoided his intense stare.

"We don't have to talk about work," Lincoln said.

I breathed a sigh of relief. Good.

"You know where I'm from. It seems you have me at a disadvantage. Where are you from? New York, Los Angeles, somewhere else?"

"Just outside of L.A.," I said. "Have you lived here all your life? Do you live in a cabin in the woods?" He looked like the type who avoided civilization.

Lincoln laughed and placed the half-empty glass of beer on the counter beside him. "I'm well-traveled, and I spent quite a bit of time in the military, but I've always called Montana home."

"You were in the military?" I repeated, surprised by his look. I always thought military guys kept their crew cuts, but it was a stereotype.

Lincoln's eyes softened as he spoke. "It's been a few years, but I was in the army, special forces."

"Wow. That's impressive." It was no wonder he was built like a statue, perfect in every possible way.

I finished the last of my screwdriver and reached out, my hand touching his bicep. He really was thick. "I wonder what else is thick," I said under my breath.

Lincoln stared at me.

"Your muscles are thick," I stammered.

Shit.

Could I blabber on any more and embarrass myself further?

"You're hot."

Apparently so.

I needed to shut up, but I didn't seem capable of it. The words just kept spilling out past my lips.

He took another swig of his beer, and I made sure every drop was gone from my screwdriver before I gestured over the bartender for another drink.

Lincoln shook his head no. "I think you've exceeded your limit."

"I don't usually drink," I said.

The room swayed a bit, but more than anything, my gaze was on him. It was as if he was the only one in existence, and nothing else mattered.

I pinched the bridge of my nose. "You may be right. I should probably go back to the hotel."

As much as I wanted him to join me, I wasn't comfortable inviting him over to my place.

I may have wanted to be *that* girl, but I wasn't her.

"How about I give you a lift home?" He gestured the bartender over to close our tabs and ring us out.

A sheepish grin crossed my face. "I don't think that's a good idea."

"You driving is an even worse one," Lincoln said.

He was right, but luckily my motel was across the street and didn't require me to get behind the wheel of a car. "I'm staying just over there," I said, motioning with my hand.

The bartender slid a receipt and pen to me to sign, along with my credit card. We both closed our tabs.

He mumbled something under his breath.

"What's that?" I asked.

I signed the receipt, my signature a bunch of curls and scribbles, illegible, and I shoved my credit card back into my wallet.

Was he grumbling over the cost of drinks or where I had booked a room?

"I'll walk you home," Lincoln said.

If he wanted to accompany me across the street in the dark, I'd accept that proposition, but that was all I was willing to accept. "Knock yourself out."

I wasn't inviting him into my room for drinks or other scandalous acts. It was dark outside and walking alone in a small town in the middle of nowhere probably wasn't a wise decision.

I slid off the stool, my feet planted firmly on the ground, but my body swayed. I'd had one too many screwdrivers: two.

"Whoa, there," Lincoln said. He was quick to put an arm around my waist to steady me.

While I enjoyed his touch, I also didn't want him to get the impression that I was interested in more, at least not right now.

I'd just met the guy.

Well, technically, I met him earlier that morning, but it was still the same damned day.

I exhaled a breath, trying to steady myself in the bar. "I'm okay," I said and glanced at him as he stood beside me, towering over me. "You don't have to hold me up. I won't fall."

He leaned in, his breath warm, which sent tingles through my body. "If you insist," Lincoln whispered. His tight grip around my waist loosened.

I slipped from his grasp and staggered out of the bar, one foot in front of the other. I didn't tip over or fall, but he was right, I could not get behind the wheel of any vehicle.

Stepping outside into the cool spring breeze, I wrapped my arms tight around myself.

Lincoln kept up with me as he strode right along my side. He shucked off his coat. "Hold up," he said and wrapped his jacket around my shoulders. "Here."

I slid my arms into the sleeves, already warmer. He had long sleeves on and had been smart in what he wore. "Thank you," I said and pulled the lightweight coat tighter.

I shouldn't have borrowed his jacket. The smell of his masculine scent was intoxicating as it enveloped my senses.

I took in a long, deep inhale, breathing his scent in, my body warm and tingling.

"Everything okay?" Lincoln asked with a raised eyebrow.

Shit.

Had he noticed what I'd done?

No. He couldn't have.

I shoved my hands into his coat pockets, my fingers warmer already. Together, we strode across the quiet road for the motel.

Why was the parking lot jam-packed with vehicles? The motel hadn't been crowded earlier when I'd checked into the place. Had the rooms all been booked over the past couple of hours?

A flash of bright light in the darkness blinded me.

I held up my arm to shield my face and my identity. "Fuck," I said with a groan and stopped walking.

I'd been caught.

CHAPTER THREE

JAXSON

"Nice of Lincoln to offer to get us drinks," I said. Our friend and newest member of the Eagle Tactical team had disappeared to the bar and hadn't returned.

I'd have worried if I hadn't noticed that he sat perched on a stool, talking up the cute little blonde.

I tended to be observant in nature. My military training factored into the equation, but I failed to notice the blonde on her approach. Only that she had sat on a stool beside him.

Had he offered to grab us drinks because he wanted to speak to her?

Or had she snuck up and spoken to him first?

Ariella sat across from me.

The giant booth felt cold and lonely. I wanted her on my lap, curled up against my body. That would have to wait until later.

Tonight.

In the privacy of my home.

It was complicated.

I was Ariella's boss, and we'd made a rule of no fraternizing.

Obviously, it hadn't lasted. It'd been too difficult for me to work around her and live with her. The living arrangements had happened before we were involved.

Well, kind of.

We had slept together, and then her house burned down.

Seeing as how I was her next-door neighbor, I offered to let her stay. One night turned into two.

She couldn't afford to live anywhere else, and she was great with my daughter Izzie.

Hiding our relationship from the guys, though, that was the hardest thing I've ever done.

But I didn't see another choice. Ariella needed the job, and I needed *her*.

Mason grumbled under his breath as he sat beside Hazel and me next to him.

"What's that?" I asked, glancing at Mason.

"I want a drink—a really stiff, hard shot of something. Anything," Mason said.

Hazel patted his good arm, the one that hadn't been shot recently.

Mason was still recovering; albeit he had been home from the hospital for six weeks, but it took time to heal and recuperate.

It seemed he was getting a little stir crazy, not that I could blame him. I didn't think I could handle being cooped up at my house for six weeks, either.

He nudged Hazel beside him. "Are you really going to tell me I can't have one drink?"

"That's right, tough guy." Her hand slipped onto his thigh, and I averted my gaze. "No alcohol until you get the all-clear from the doctor. You have an appointment tomorrow, and if he says you can drink like a fish, then I'll bring you all the liquor that you want."

"He's not going to say that," I said. There was no way his physician would make that statement.

Hazel ran a hand through Mason's hair, pushing the long dark strands out of his eyes. "How about I grab you something special from the bar, a sweet virgin treat?"

"Are you trying to tease me," Mason groaned.

Hazel planted a kiss on his cheek before she climbed over Ariella and headed out of the booth to the bar.

"I'll give her a hand," I offered and scooted out from the opposite side of the booth.

I followed Hazel to the bar, on the opposite side of where Lincoln and the pretty girl were situated.

She almost looked familiar, but I wasn't sure why.

Hazel leaned against the counter and gestured over the bartender. The bar was busy, crowded, which was unusual for a Sunday night.

A few locals sat at the bar, but most of the tables were unfamiliar faces, and for a small town, that was unusual, especially out of tourist season.

Was there an event happening at the Blue Sky Resort? On occasion, there'd been conferences held off-season that had booked out every room in the place and brought tourists to all the local spots.

"Do you recognize her?" Hazel asked, her eyes on the blonde Lincoln chatted up.

I exhaled a heavy sigh. "It's like she's familiar, but I'm not sure from where."

The bartender finally stepped over, and we ordered two pitchers of beer along with a virgin daiquiri for Mason.

I handed over my credit card to the bartender while he rang up the orders.

"Mason's going to kill you," I whispered into Hazel's ear. I'd never known the man to drink anything girly in my life, let alone non-alcoholic.

Hazel grinned as she turned to face me. "Why? I told him he'd get a sweet virgin treat. Obviously, it's not me."

My eyes widened, and I glanced back toward the bartender. "That was more information than I needed."

I should have ordered myself something stronger tonight than beer if I was going to have to listen to Hazel and Mason's flirtations.

"Oh, come on. I see the way you and Ariella gaze at each other. You should ask her to dance," Hazel said.

"We're colleagues. More importantly, I'm her boss."

Hazel didn't have the slightest notion that Ariella and I were involved.

Right?

The bartender handed me the receipt, and I signed the slip of paper before he handed me two pitchers of beer.

I brought the pitchers back to the table while Hazel carried the strawberry daiquiri to the table and placed it in front of Mason.

"You have got to be kidding me," Mason said. He didn't look the least bit thrilled with the slushy sitting on the table in front of him.

"If you don't drink it, I will," Hazel said.

Mason pushed the glass across the table to Hazel. "Have at it."

I headed back to the bar to grab a stack of clear plastic cups for the beer.

"Need a hand?" Ariella's soft, warm voice caught me off guard as she stood behind me.

I spun around and handed her a few cups while I carried the rest to the table. "Sure." I appreciated her help. "Thank you."

It was painstakingly hard to sit across from her for a fun night out and not touch her, taste her, feel her body nestled up against mine—pure torture.

I planted the plastic cups on the table and grabbed Ariella's hand before she could sit back down.

Ariella had already dropped the cups on the table, and Hazel started handing them out and pouring beer into each one.

"Dance with me," I said, taking Hazel's advice. If she didn't think it was a big deal, then maybe the guys wouldn't, either.

Ariella's eyes widened. "Jaxson," she whispered, keeping her voice low and quiet.

It was difficult to hear her over the loud pulsating sound of music that played overhead on the speaker system.

"It's not karaoke night. I'm not asking you to sing with me."

"If you do, I'll kill you," Ariella said. "Even Izzie knows I don't sing."

I laughed under my breath. She'd heard me sing Izzie to bed a few times, and while I wasn't anything special in the vocals department, I could carry a tune —mostly.

"Then dance with me," I said and gave her hand a firm squeeze.

It was just a dance.

Everyone at Eagle Tactical knew there was chemistry between us.

There was no harm in dancing.

I'd found it hard enough to keep my hands to myself at the office, but there hadn't been another choice. Bending her over my desk and taking her the way I wanted was hardly classified as professional.

I yanked her closer.

She groaned and let me pull her tight against my body.

"Am I going to have to dance with all my work colleagues?" Ariella asked. "Because I'm not comfortable getting that intimate with Declan, Aiden, Mason, or Lincoln."

Laughing, I pulled her close and tight against my body. "Just me."

"Good, because I don't want to feel any of them bump up against me," Ariella whispered into my ear.

She wrapped her arms around my neck, her fingers warm against my skin.

Staring into her eyes, I wanted to kiss her, but I couldn't, not with the others watching.

There wasn't a corner, a hallway to sneak in and steal her away for a few kisses and intimate moments together.

"I want to take you home, have my way with you, Freckles." Every ounce of strength within me was focused on controlling my impulses.

I had to break my gaze and glance away. The temptation of *her* was just too damned much.

Her scent.

The feel of her warm body pressed tight against me.

I needed her.

Lincoln stood and helped the young blonde to her feet.

I guess he wasn't joining us tonight. That was fine with me. I wasn't sure how much longer I'd want to stay out at the bar and keep my hands to myself.

"Do you want to get out of here?" I whispered into her ear.

Freckles smiled and laughed at me, pulling back only slightly. "I do, but we can't. Lincoln has bailed, and Mason needs a friend, so does Hazel."

"They've got Aiden and Declan." Those guys were still single, as far as I knew. If they were dating anyone recently, they hadn't mentioned it.

"You're going to suggest we leave Hazel with the three of them? That poor girl has been tending to Mason for a month."

"Longer," I said.

"What?"

"It's been longer than a month. Six weeks that she's played nurse to his injuries." Mason hadn't been one to divulge any dirty details about what did or didn't happen between the two of them.

"Playing nurse?" Ariella let her hands slide down my back, holding me close as we danced intimately. "This is the first I'm hearing about it."

"Would she tell you?"

"Probably not," Ariella said, a bright smile on her face. She squinted up at me. "We should probably head back to the table. You should offer to dance with Hazel."

"Why?" It was Hazel's idea that I dance with Ariella, not that I hadn't thought about it, but I wasn't sure it was a good idea.

She untangled from around me, and the room felt several degrees chillier.

Ariella sauntered back to the booth and scooted back in to sit.

I sat down beside Mason and reached for the beer on the table that hadn't been touched.

Hazel cleared her throat, a huge grin plastered to her face. "You're not going to ask me to dance? I could use some of that bump and grind action."

I nearly spit my beer out of my mouth, coughing at her words.

My phone buzzed in my pocket, and I dug in and reached for it to answer. Anything to get out of that conversation with Hazel. Next, she'd probably ask me if Ariella and I were sleeping together.

"Eagle Tactical?" I answered the caller and stood, taking the phone with me as I headed outside, where it was quiet, and I could hear what was being said.

"Hi, yes. I'd like to inquire about your security services. We are looking to contract out security for our on-location production shoot in your area, beginning tomorrow."

"You do realize we're in Breckenridge, Montana." I hadn't heard about any film production taking place in our town.

News like that would have traveled fast.

"Yes, our studio manager was supposed to contact you, but it appears he neglected to do so. I apologize for the late notice, but we need a full team of security to staff us during filming, and our insurance policy requires that our feature star have a bodyguard."

I exhaled a heavy sigh. "How many security personnel do you require onsite during filming?" I asked.

"A team of four or five should be adequate in addition to someone who will babysit Harper Madison. I'll text you over her picture along with the location for production, which begins tomorrow morning. I should warn you. Miss Madison does not —how do I put this kindly—appreciate the length that the studio goes to ensure her safety. It is required that she is not aware of your services."

"That isn't how we work," I said.

We couldn't protect her if she didn't want us around.

"I'm not asking, sir. The contract will stipulate that Miss Madison is not to be made aware of her protective detail by any party within or employed by your company."

"And if I say no?"

"That isn't an option."

CHAPTER FOUR

LINCOLN

I'd never seen the motel parking lot crammed with so many vehicles, cars, trucks, and vans.

"There she is!" a man shouted from across the road as he stood outside the motel.

A bright flash of light erupted once, twice, and before I could count how many more times, I realized Harper had stopped walking and shielded her face.

Vehicle doors began opening and slamming shut.

Men on foot with cameras and camcorders rushed toward us.

"Quick, my truck." I grabbed her free hand that wasn't shielding herself and hurried her to my truck.

I dug my keys out of my pocket as we rushed to the passenger side. I opened the door for her and slammed it shut as the men poured into the bar parking lot.

Who the hell were they? I didn't wait around to ask or find out.

I jogged around to the driver's side, climbed into the truck, and started the engine.

"Please get me out of here." Her voice quivered as she spoke.

She didn't need to tell me twice.

Yanking on my seatbelt, I put the truck into reverse, hightailing it out of the parking lot, my wheels squealing in the process.

"Thank you." Her words were soft. Her voice seemed fragile.

I left a trail of dust behind me as we drove away from the bar in a hurry. No one followed us, at least not yet. I took the mountain pass north. "Where do you want me to take you?"

Her motel had been a shitty dump. The place was known for bedbugs and not many visitors. How it stayed open was beyond me.

"Someplace quiet where they won't find me."

Who exactly were *they*?

Paparazzi?

I drove north on the mountain pass and headed for the restaurant. The place was quiet and deserted. There wouldn't be anyone stopping by or bothering us.

"Sure." I didn't push with questions. At least not yet.

Every so often, I glanced in the rearview mirror, making sure that we weren't being followed.

In the distance, headlights shined in my rearview mirror. I hit the gas harder, pushing up the mountain faster. Thankfully, the snow had recently melted, and while there had been some muddy days, the weather had been dry and sunny recently.

I turned off the mountain pass toward the restaurant and shut off the headlights.

"How can you see?" Harper asked, staring at the road in front of us.

I couldn't see a damned thing. I slowed to a crawl but didn't stop. I needed to be careful.

I'd driven this path thousands of times in the dark, but never without headlights. I inched forward, familiar with the path.

Trees surrounded us on both sides of the road, making it difficult to see anything in front of us. The new moon offered no light, but the trees would have hidden it anyhow.

I waited.

An engine roared behind us and passed the driveway.

Another minute, when I was confident the traveler couldn't see us, I flipped on my headlights and proceeded down the trail toward the restaurant.

Harper exhaled a heavy sigh.

"Don't worry. You're safe here." I pulled the truck up out front of the restaurant and shut off the engine. "Come on. Let's get you inside."

She followed out of the truck and behind me up the porch steps of the restaurant.

I unlocked the front door and flipped on the lights. I hurried to the shades, closing them, making sure that no one would see us inside, and while I didn't intend on hanging out downstairs, I didn't want to take any chances.

"Wow," Harper whispered. She stood by the front door and shut it after she stepped inside.

I closed another shade, the curtains darkened the building from the outside. "Make sure you lock the door."

Harper turned on her heels and secured the deadbolt before she stepped farther into the restaurant. "What happened here?"

"Long story," I said. With the last of the curtains shut, I glanced around, satisfied she wouldn't be seen.

With her eyebrow raised, she stared at me.

Was she waiting for me to elaborate? She wasn't the most forthcoming with the men chasing us with cameras. I assumed they were paparazzi, but I wasn't sure.

I'd never been chased by men with cameras, only men with guns.

She shrugged out of my coat and slowly let it slide off her shoulders before she held it out to me.

I took the coat from her grasp and carried it with me toward the staircase.

"Are you coming?" I called after her.

I didn't turn around.

The soft patter of her footsteps was her answer.

She followed me up the stairwell and into my apartment. Harper cleared her throat.

I flipped on the lights and made sure the curtains upstairs were shut too. I closed the living room blinds that peeked out to the parking lot of the restaurant. While I wasn't expecting visitors, I also didn't want to chance it. Clearly, she didn't want to be seen or found.

"Have a seat," I said and gestured toward the leather sofa.

She slunk down into the supple material. Slipping out of her shoes, she drew her legs up beside her body. Her eyes were heavy.

Had she been exhausted, or was it the alcohol that made her sleepy?

"Thank you." Her eyelids fluttered closed momentarily before they bounced back open. "You're probably wondering what all that was about earlier, at the motel."

I opened the wooden trunk my grandmother had given me and retrieved a throw blanket, offering it to her.

Harper's hand stretched out, clutching the cotton before she pulled it over her legs. She seemed to relax under the warmth of the blanket.

"You don't owe me an explanation," I said. I wasn't going to push her. If she wanted to tell me, she would.

Her eyelids fluttered closed again. This time she yawned and pulled the blanket higher toward her chin as she stretched out on the sofa.

I told her I'd grab a pillow to make her more comfortable if she wanted to crash here for the night.

"I do," Harper said, a half-mumble. Her words seemed to slur together as she spoke. "The paparazzi are always after me. Thank you, Lincoln. You're too kind."

"Happy to help," I said and let out a heavy sigh. I hadn't intended to invite her up to my place to sleep, but she was just about out already.

Attempting to be quiet, I strode down the hall and to the linen closet, retrieving a spare pillow. I brought it back out to the living room only to discover Harper softly snoring, stretched out, asleep on the sofa.

I bent down to her level, not wanting to startle her. "I brought you a pillow," I said in a soft, soothing tone, guiding her head up just a bit and the pillow under her neck to make sure that she was comfortable.

"Thank you," she mumbled.

I shut off the lights and quietly stalked to my bedroom.

My phone buzzed in my pocket, and I glanced down at the dozens of text messages that I'd missed from my friends, the guys at Eagle Tactical.

It would have to wait.

I'd answer them tomorrow morning when I knew more about what was going on, assuming she'd tell me.

————

Early the next morning, my phone buzzed beside me on the nightstand, waking me at the crack of dawn.

"Yeah. It's Lincoln," I said, answering the caller. I hadn't even noticed who had called on the caller I.D. since I'd been half-asleep when I answered the phone.

"I'm downstairs in your restaurant. Can you come down?"

"Jaxson?" What was he doing visiting with me on a Monday morning?

Did we have a new client? That was the only thing that made sense.

But why show up and not just call me?

"Yes, get dressed and come downstairs."

I ran a hand through my hair. "Yeah. I'll be down in a second." I ended the call and tossed my cell phone onto my mattress.

Stumbling around the bedroom in the dark, I grabbed a pair of jeans, a dark shirt, and socks and threw them on before I slipped on my shoes and quietly headed out of the bedroom and past the living room.

Harper was still sound asleep.

I didn't want to wake her. I hurried down the stairs, the bright light of the restaurant making my eyes burn.

Jaxson stood downstairs, leaning against the counter that had been pelted with dozens of bullets.

"Morning," Jaxson said. "I came up to visit but saw you had company."

I ran a hand through my tousled hair.

"Yeah. Busy night." I didn't want to elaborate, and while Jaxson may have thought something happened between me and the girl I left with at the bar, I wasn't going to confirm or deny his suspicions.

I don't kiss and tell.

"You could have just called," I said and folded my arms across my chest.

I needed coffee, but the brewer was shot to hell, and those little coffee pods didn't do justice.

"I texted you last night, but you didn't answer."

"Yeah, I was busy." I ran a hand through my hair and headed back to the kitchen to at least fetch a glass of water for myself. "You didn't drop by just to tell me you texted."

That wasn't at all like Jaxson. Something had come up, but I hadn't the slightest notion of what.

Jaxson followed me to the kitchen and stood in the doorway. "We have a new client. A Hollywood studio hired us as a security detail while they film a movie production over the next couple of weeks."

I lifted the glass of water to my lips and paused. "Paparazzi," I muttered under my breath.

No wonder the studio needed security. It wasn't from the townspeople of Breckenridge interfering with filming or harassing its stars.

"Yeah, probably," Jaxson said. "Mostly, they want us to keep bystanders away and make sure the stars feel safe. There's one other thing."

I finished the glass of water and placed it in the sink. "Of course, there is." There was always something else.

"The studio requested that one member of our team take on a security detail off-hours for the main movie star. I think you should be the one to handle the starlet. She's young, trouble, and you've already gotten to know her."

"What?" My head spun.

"Harper Madison. The girl upstairs in your apartment, she's the Hollywood starlet. The studio mentioned that she might not be on board with a bodyguard, but it's a requirement for the film to get financed and the insurance company to greenlight the picture. Apparently, she has a knack for getting into trouble."

Shit.

It was too early to hear this about Harper. "You don't say."

Jaxson stepped closer. "Listen, I wouldn't even ask you to do this, but I saw the way she looked at you, opened up to you, and I assume she trusts you."

"She's not going to trust me when she finds out I've been hired as her personal bodyguard," I said. She didn't seem the type to appreciate that I'd been hired to look out for her.

Maybe I was wrong, and she'd be ecstatic, but we had to keep things professional between us.

I didn't sleep with my colleagues or clients.

Jaxson exhaled a heavy breath, his jaw tight. "I suggest you don't tell her. Invite her out to dinner for tonight, after the film shoot, and tour her around town. Show her a good time but not too good of a time."

"We had a couple of drinks last night. That was it," I said.

I didn't go into detail about the men chasing her down with the cameras outside of her shitty motel room.

Did Jaxson need to hear about that? Maybe if he was her security detail, but he was putting me in charge.

"I know. I came upstairs and didn't figure a girl sleeping on your couch was someone you slept with. It's why I trust you with this security detail."

Great.

As much as I wanted it to be me, I also wasn't ready for the drama that would ensue. "You want me to be her bodyguard."

She was going to kill me.

I just had to make sure that she never found out that I'd been hired to protect her.

"Yes." Jaxson grew silent as we heard the upstairs door squeak and shut.

Harper was awake and on her way downstairs.

Jaxson stepped around the corner and into the kitchen and nodded for me to step out into the restaurant.

Her soft footsteps trampled over the wooden floorboards.

"Good morning," I said, greeting her.

She had cleaned up pretty well for sleeping on a sofa all night and having one too many drinks.

"Morning. Do you mind driving me back to the motel? I need to get my car."

"Sure." I dug into my pocket for my keys and led her outside, locking up behind myself.

I glanced once more in the direction of the kitchen where Jaxson had stashed himself.

I led Harper out to my truck. Beside it this morning, Ariella's sedan had been parked and abandoned.

"Whose vehicle is that?" Harper asked. She climbed into the front seat and glanced around.

Was she worried that it was more paparazzi out looking for her?

"Just one of the guys helping me fix up the restaurant." It wasn't a complete lie. Jaxson had mentioned how he wouldn't mind doing some renovations on the inside.

Why the hell had he taken Ariella's car?

I put the truck into reverse and headed back on the road we came in on last night.

Harper sat quietly, staring out the window. "Can I ask you something?"

"Sure." I had a feeling she was going to either way.

"What happened to your restaurant? Those bullet holes aren't for décor."

I snorted under my breath. "That's a new one. And no, they are one hundred percent real."

That story would take some time, and maybe it would buy me the opportunity to see her later tonight when I was working and keeping an eye on her.

"It's a long story. How about I tell you about it tonight over dinner?"

"I have to work, but I'll text you when I leave. It might be a little late," Harper said.

"That's fine." I contemplated digging out my cell phone and handing it to her to punch in her number, but I thought better of it. What if she read the texts about the studio security job that had been lined up with Eagle Tactical?

"Pull out your phone. I'll give you my number." I waited for her to retrieve her cell phone, and I recited my digits so that she'd be able to get ahold of me later.

A few minutes later, we were pulling up out front of the motel. The parking lot was nearly empty, unlike last night.

In the distance, I recognized Aiden's truck.

He was staking out the motel parking lot. At least Harper would be safe.

I needed to head home and shower. As long as I didn't have to be onset, then she'd never know I worked for Eagle Tactical.

CHAPTER FIVE

ARIELLA

I rubbed the sleep from my tired eyes and stumbled into the kitchen, the bright lights and wide-open blinds casting in the morning light.

I squinted.

My eyes didn't adjust fast enough and made it difficult to see.

My autonomic nervous system sucked. I was one of the unlucky few with a disorder that doctors struggled to understand.

"Are you okay?" Jaxson's warm voice met my ears as he wrapped his arms around my waist, steadying me.

My body melted into his embrace, his touch warm and inviting.

I didn't want to get ready for work.

"Just my vision." I could feel his look, the concern weighing heavily on both of us. "I'm fine. It's nothing."

The last thing I wanted was to worry him.

I wanted to climb back into bed, more specifically *his* bed, but we were careful. With Skylar visiting indefinitely and his little girl constantly inviting herself into the bedroom, I'd slept in the guest room more nights than I liked.

"Just your vision?" Jaxson repeated. "I don't like the sound of that." He backed me up several feet, cradling me against the cabinets.

His body trapped mine.

"Jaxson?"

He raised his right hand up to my eye level. "How many fingers am I holding up?" he asked.

My eyes had already adjusted by the time he'd trapped me against the counter, but I hadn't wanted to admit it.

I liked being pressed up tight against him, his guard down as he focused on me.

"Ariella?" He sounded worried that I hadn't answered him fast enough.

"Three fingers," I said. "My vision just takes a little longer to adjust than other people's does. Bright lights or going from a dark room to somewhere bright is difficult, and heaven help me if I go back to a dark room right after."

He brushed a strand of hair behind my ear, his touch stirring a desire he fueled within me.

"What happens then?" Jaxson asked. His fingers played in my hair and slid against my neck as he held me close.

I wanted to kiss him, but we had agreed to take things slow around Izzie and Skylar, not to mention we were hiding our relationship from our work colleagues, the guys at Eagle Tactical.

"I start seeing these weird shapes, and it makes me nauseous."

Skylar breezed into the kitchen, oblivious to the intimate moment between us. "I get those too. Auras are the worst. Well, technically, the migraines are the worst, but I can't stand when I get one of those visual trips," Skylar said.

Jaxson untangled his hand and pulled it away before he stepped back from within my personal space.

I whimpered in protest, and he locked eyes with me.

I hated that we had to play this game, a dance of what we could and couldn't do around others. I wanted to throw my arms around him, plant my lips on his, and not worry about who saw us or what they thought or felt. We were grown adults.

"Are you having an aura now?" Jaxson asked.

"No, I'm fine now. Thank you."

Skylar glared at me.

What had I done to piss her off? Was she ever planning on moving out of her brother's house?

"Any word from Mason?" I asked, trying desperately to change the subject.

Jaxson reached for his coffee and took a sip. "He's got a doctor's appointment this afternoon. He is hoping he gets the all clear from the doc and can come back into the office tomorrow."

I brushed past him for the cabinet that held the mugs and retrieved one for myself. "How likely is that?" I asked, pouring myself a steaming cup of coffee.

He'd been hit by two bullets. It took time to heal, but how much time did he need? "He seemed like he was doing well last night."

"It could go either way," Jaxson said. "I'll be glad to have him back, but yeah, he did seem like he was having a good time last night, which reminds me, I need to swing by Lincoln's place this morning before work."

"Oh?" I had no idea what he needed to discuss with him before work, but it wasn't any of my business. "Do you want me to get Izzie ready this morning and take her to daycare?" I asked. I'd picked her up a few times recently for him, so I'd become familiar with their routine.

"That would be really helpful," Jaxson said. He dropped a quick, chaste kiss to my cheek.

I froze, surprised by his gesture.

What if Izzie came running into the kitchen?

While we both knew that Skylar was aware of our relationship, we'd tried to be discreet around Isabella. Jaxson hadn't wanted to confuse his daughter and the fact I was already living under his roof... well, it wasn't helping matters, either.

"Can you secure her car seat in my vehicle?" I asked.

"I'll do you one better, take my truck today," Jaxson said.

"Are you sure?" He'd never offered for me to drive his truck before.

Didn't he worry about the Eagle Tactical guys saying something? Although they all knew I was living with Jaxson, that was because my house next door had burned down.

How long could that excuse last?

"I trust you with my daughter, Freckles. You can guarantee that she rates above my truck."

I took a long sip of my coffee. My cheeks felt hot under his stare.

"I need you to join me in the field today. Our newest client requires the entire team for their assignment," he said, sipping his coffee as he glanced at Skylar. It was clear he wasn't comfortable discussing specifics in front of her. "With Mason unavailable, I need you in the field instead of the office today."

I had so many questions, but he shook his head, silently telling me not to ask them right now. "Okay."

My stomach bubbled with nervousness.

What would I be required to do in the field? I wasn't a field agent, even with my time at the C.I.A.. I always stayed behind a desk or buried behind a computer in a hotel room.

"I'll be texting the team the meetup point. Just come by as soon as you're done dropping off Izzie at daycare."

My breath caught in my throat. "Sure."

Jaxson stepped closer.

Had he sensed my hesitation?

He rested a strong, warm hand on my upper arm. "You've got this, Freckles. I promise I wouldn't include you in the field assignment if I didn't believe you were ready for it."

I offered him a weak smile. "I appreciate it." Which was true, even though I felt sick at the thought of what I had to do, and I wasn't even sure what would be involved.

"You look like you're going to be sick," Jaxson muttered. With a heavy sigh, he grabbed my hand and pulled me into the bathroom, shutting the door.

"Jaxson?" What was he doing?

"Breathe," he said as his blue eyes stared right into mine.

I exhaled a heavy breath that I hadn't realized I'd been holding.

Jaxson clasped my hands tight, and I glanced down at our joined hands. Mine trembled. "You got this, Freckles." He held one hand tight and flipped on the bathroom fan with the other hand.

"Do I?" I asked, my voice squeaking. I grimaced and exhaled a long breath, trying to calm myself. "I'm not a field agent. I work well in an office, where there's stability and structure."

He wrapped his strong arms around my waist and pulled me tight against his body. "Just imagine that you're doing office work outside," Jaxson said.

His breath teased my neck, and his lips caressed my skin. Slowly, he dropped soft kisses just behind my ear.

He was my undoing—each and every time.

"You got this, Freckles," Jaxson said again.

I exhaled a heavy breath through my nose. My eyes shut, I nodded. "Give it to me. What's the assignment?"

He'd brought me into the bathroom to tell me, right? Out of earshot of Skylar, who had a big mouth.

"There's a film crew starting this morning for a movie. They're requesting a security team to monitor the production and make sure that no one uninvited breaches the set."

"That's it?" I breathed a sigh of relief. "Now I feel like an idiot."

"Don't," Jaxson said. "You can't help how you feel or how your body responds." He pulled me tight against him, one hand on my lower back, the other cradling my ass.

I smiled and leaned in, stealing a kiss, unsure when I'd get the opportunity again with him. Just the two of us, alone.

———

I'd never done security detail, but Jaxson needed an extra body, and while I didn't look the least bit threatening, I could at least make sure no one ran on set who didn't belong. Plus, I had a walkie-talkie, and I was to report to Jaxson anyone whom I deemed suspicious.

I wasn't expecting much to happen.

No one knew a film crew was scheduled in town, but people would talk when they noticed side roads were closed and the cast trailers parked out on the open field just off the main road.

The locals would come, curious about the production in a town of less than a thousand.

While I hadn't lived in Breckenridge for long, this was probably the most exciting thing to happen in the spring months, when skiing and snowboarding were closed for the season.

It was difficult to tear my gaze from Jaxson.

While he stood guard outside of the cast's trailer, specifically Harper Madison's, my responsibility was to make sure that the crew members all wore badges to easily be identified.

The job was easy for the most part, making sure no one snuck on set who didn't belong.

Did anyone even realize outside of the production crew that Harper Madison was in town?

She probably stayed under a fake name at whatever hotel she had checked into.

When the stars paused for lunch, I grabbed a quick bite to eat in my car, enjoying the solitude. I couldn't join Jaxson for lunch as much as I wanted to because we both couldn't afford to take an hour off at the same time.

Finishing a quick meal, I strode across the parking lot, back toward the set.

A sharp pinch struck my neck.

I reached up to rub away the pain, and my vision blurred. I opened my mouth to scream when I felt a hand cover my lips.

My body slumped, about to fall to the ground, when a set of arms lifted me into their embrace.

Darkness swept over me.

CHAPTER SIX

HARPER

I wanted a real home-cooked meal or at least something tasty, not the craft services deli spread that had been set out for the cast and crew to dine on during filming.

While I appreciated their effort, I wanted to steal an hour for myself away from the set.

I stepped out from my trailer, my purse on my shoulder, donning a pair of sunglasses.

I avoided the security team, a bunch of good-looking guys who were locals, former military, and they looked every bit ready to kick some ass.

If I hadn't met Lincoln the night before, I might have considered flirting with one of them, but truthfully, that was all an act.

How I wanted to be, not who I was as a person.

I snatched a baseball cap that had been abandoned on a nearby chair and tucked my long blonde hair under the cap, trying to disguise myself as best as I could.

No one seemed to notice me, dressed like everyone else. With their attention elsewhere, I slipped offset and out to the parking lot, a mowed field, for my rental car.

The hair on my arms stood on end.

A woman with long dark hair slumped over, and a gentleman caught her from behind and swooped her into his arms.

He carried her across the parking lot.

"Hey!" I shouted, rushing after the gentleman.

What the hell was going on?

Was she okay?

I didn't get a close enough glance to see if she was someone I knew from filming.

He carried her toward a white van. "Mind your own business," a gruff voice retorted.

He yanked open the back door of his vehicle.

I hurried after them and shoved my hand into my purse. I yanked out my hot pink can of mace and held it up, threatening the abductor.

Everything told me she was in danger, that whoever this guy was, he was out to hurt her.

"Let her go!" I screamed, hoping that someone would hear my shouts.

Where the hell was the security team who was hired to watch the set?

He wasn't the least bit gentle with the brunette as he tossed her into the back of the van.

The moment he turned around, I had my finger on the trigger of the mace, but he ripped it from my petite hands and backhanded me across the face.

My cheek stung, and my eyes burned with fear.

"Get in." He nodded toward the open back door where the young woman lay motionless.

Was she asleep?

Dead?

"No, I'm not going anywhere with you." I took a step back, unsure how to help the woman in the van. If I went with her, I'd be endangering my life.

I wasn't brave.

I wasn't fearless.

I was an actress, and while I could play a part, it involved lines and scripts. I couldn't play this part, not the one where I appeared strong.

He grabbed me by the waist and tossed me into the back of the van.

"No!" I shrieked and lunged at the man, my fingernails digging into his eyes and forcing him to stumble backward. I used the moment to my advantage and flung myself out of the van and past him, tripping over my feet.

I slammed into the grass, eating dirt.

"You bitch!" the perpetrator snarled and reached into the van.

I wasn't about to wait around to find out whether he drew a gun or something else at me.

I hurried to my feet and rushed between cars, ducking so that he couldn't see me. I kept low to the ground, listening for his footsteps or the heavy breaths that he took, panting for air.

As much as I wanted to help the woman in the van, the best thing I could do for her now was to get help.

If he had a gun, I would be outmatched.

I stayed low to the ground and hurried through the crowded parking lot back toward the production set.

Tires squealed and kicked up dirt as I lifted my head. The white van high-tailed it out of the parking lot.

I didn't bother needing to duck any longer or hide from the perpetrator.

I was free, but she wasn't.

CHAPTER SEVEN

JAXSON

Harper came running up to me, her cheeks red, the sunglasses she wore pushed back on her head, a baseball cap in her trembling hand.

"Help!" Harper came barreling back onset, glancing from one side of the set to the other, looking for someone.

I hurried over, unsure what was bothering her.

Had they run out of tiny sandwiches on the lunch table?

She looked frantic and panicked, but I couldn't even fathom what had gotten her quite so worked up.

"What can I help you with?" I asked calmly, trying to ease whatever anxiety she was experiencing.

"He took her!" she gasped, with widened eyes as she pointed behind herself at the parking lot.

"Whoa, slow down. Can you tell me what you saw?" I gestured Aiden over.

I couldn't see Ariella or Declan from where I was positioned.

Aiden jogged over, sensing the urgency.

He didn't say a word, just listened.

"I was heading out to my car," Harper said, "and this guy, kinda big, taller than me, dark hair and dark eyes, was carrying a girl to his van, a white van. She was unconscious. At least I hope that's all it was and she wasn't dead."

I swallowed the lump forming in my throat. "Did you get a license plate?" I asked.

Harper shook her head no.

I hoped this wasn't a game or publicity stunt that she was trying to pull, but the quiver in her voice made me trust her.

"He tried to grab me too, so I fought back and ran," Harper said.

"Good." I exhaled a long slow breath. "Do you know the girl he took?"

She shook her head. "I didn't recognize her, but I'm not always great with remembering people. The girl had long dark hair. I'm sorry, I wish I could be of more help." Harper chewed on her bottom lip. "Can we do a roll call or something on set?"

"That's not a terrible idea," Aiden said. "There are no cameras on the parking lot."

"Did either of them have any distinguishing marks?" I asked, trying to jog her memory before it became even more clouded and faded with time.

"No. I don't remember anything special."

"What about facial hair?" I asked. "Was he wearing glasses? Any tattoos?"

"Definitely no glasses. I poked his eyes when I tried to get away. I don't remember any facial hair or tattoos."

"That's good," I said.

Aiden dug out his phone and called the local sheriff's department. We needed to report the abduction and hopefully get a team who could scour the area along with a helicopter in the sky to find the white van.

After he hung up, I met his stare. "Find Ariella. Have her and Declan set up a roster that we can go down name by name and find out who is unaccounted for."

"Who is Ariella?" Harper asked.

"One of us, part of the Eagle Tactical team," I said, not elaborating any further.

Harper's eyes widened as she pointed toward the parking lot. "Long dark hair, about the same size and build as me?"

I pulled my phone from my pocket.

"Do you have a picture of her?" she asked.

"Already on it," I said, unlocking my phone.

I opened the photos and scrolled through a few of Izzie before I landed on one with Ariella braiding Izzie's hair as they sat on the sofa together.

"Here." I held my breath, hoping it was anyone else who had been taken and not *her*.

Harper tapped the phone screen. "That definitely was the girl I saw carried into the van."

I flipped through my phone and opened a web browser before I typed in Benjamin Ryan.

Could he have shown up in Breckenridge?

He'd said on the news that he was going to reconnect with his wife, but I never expected this type of reunion.

Had he shown signs of violence in the past?

Ariella hadn't mentioned it to me. She had made it clear that it was over between them.

Had that been the reason why?

"What about this guy? Was he the one driving the van?" I showed Harper my phone screen with a picture of Benjamin Ryan. It hadn't been hard to dig up his mug shot.

Harper nodded. "You know who it is?" She seemed to breathe a sigh of relief. "That means you can help find her, right?"

"Yeah, I know of him. Never met the guy." I wasn't looking forward to meeting him now, either. "You should get back on set. I need to make a phone call and take care of some things."

"Okay," Harper said.

She seemed lighter on her feet, less stressed with the news that we knew who the missing girl was and who'd taken her.

I didn't feel the least bit better with the news that Ariella had been abducted by Benjamin.

Where the hell would he have taken her?

Had he drugged her?

She wouldn't have willingly gone with him. Harper had mentioned that Ariella had been unconscious.

I strode across the grassy field, away from the trailers and listening ears before dialing Lincoln.

"What's up?"

"Sorry to bother you. I wouldn't if it wasn't an absolute emergency, but I need you to get down here and cover my shift. Ariella's been taken."

The weight of a boulder nestled deep in my stomach, made it difficult to breathe.

"Slow down, Monroe," Lincoln said, referring to be my last name. "Are you sure she didn't just decide to go for a nice stroll?"

I shook my head, forgetting that Lincoln couldn't see me. Grimacing, I finally answered him, kicking a wayward stone tucked into the grass. "Harper saw her getting shoved into the back of a white van."

I couldn't just stand around but leaving while working a job. I couldn't do that until we had extra coverage.

What if Benjamin was a diversion?

"Shit. I'll head over there now. I'll call Mason while I'm on the way, see if he's done with his appointment and how he made out."

"Thanks." I hadn't wanted to bother Mason, but I was fairly confident that he'd want to know what was going on.

Sirens wailed in the distance. "The sheriff should be coming by any minute."

"Good. I'm still twenty minutes away. When the film shoot wraps up for the night, the rest of the team will swing by and help with the search. Keep us posted," Lincoln said.

"Will do." I ended the call and shoved the phone back into my pocket, relieved when I saw a squad car approach.

———

The sheriff put out an APB for the white van along with a notification that the abductor Benjamin Ryan should be considered armed and dangerous with a hostage.

I needed Aiden to do his magic with the computer, hacking into every record and account that Ben had, to locate where he might have taken Ariella.

Lincoln pulled into the lot and parked his truck. He hurried over. "Any news?"

"Nothing yet," I said as we hovered around the squad car.

"Does she have her phone with her?" Lincoln asked.

"If she does, it's off, and the battery has been pulled from the device. It's not pinging a signal when we try to access her phone." We had tried everything conventional. "Ben isn't the kind of guy to hold her for ransom."

Sheriff Nelson cleared his throat. "What makes you say that?"

"I did a background run on Ariella when she first moved here, for work," I said, clarifying that I hadn't done it for any other reason. I wasn't a creep. We'd been hired to look into her past for Blue Sky Resort. "That's how I found out her relation to Ben Ryan."

Rubbing the back of my neck, I still didn't like Ben, and that was before he'd abducted his ex-wife. He'd allegedly stolen money from hundreds of other unsuspecting individuals including me.

"The same Ben Ryan who was arrested and convicted of fraud?" Sheriff Nelson asked.

News traveled far and fast.

"Yeah, but he was released."

"On good behavior? What'd he serve, a year?"

"I doubt it. Something about new evidence and the charges being dropped. The conviction was overturned."

I hadn't read the specifics yet. I'd been busy with a toddler at home, and she stole the majority of my time when I wasn't at work.

"Hold on," he said as he answered his phone and stepped away for a moment.

I wanted to chase after him, find out what was being discussed, but what good would that do? "How's Harper?" Lincoln asked.

"She's fine. She's filming a scene," I said, gesturing toward the set. She was the last person on my mind right now.

Sheriff Nelson strode over to us. "We have a possible location. His phone may be off, but he used his credit card. He just checked into Blue Sky Resort."

Seriously?

Could he be any more of an idiot? At least that meant they hadn't traveled far.

"I'm calling for backup," the sheriff said, "and we're going in lights and sirens off. You want to ride with me or bring your truck?"

"I'll ride with you." I didn't want to admit that I didn't have the keys to my truck. I'd given them to Ariella earlier that morning. It was information the sheriff didn't need to have, but there'd be questions if I drove her car to the resort.

"Let us know what happens," Lincoln said. He patted me on the back before strolling onto the set.

I jumped into the passenger side of the squad car, and the sheriff jetted us out of the lot and onto the main road toward the resort.

My foot tapped against the floorboards, restless.

"We'll be there soon," he said. He flipped his lights on to hurry through traffic but left the siren off.

As we approached the last half mile, he turned off the lights and pulled into the parking lot with a half dozen other squad cars behind us.

We had to be careful.

The last time we all were here, there'd been a hostage situation, and while it had been different, I didn't want Ariella's life in jeopardy again.

"I should make you wait in the car," Sheriff Nelson said. He stepped outside, and I followed.

I had pissed him off the last time, storming in and saving Ariella and Hazel without thinking.

I'd been reckless, but I'd done what I had to do, and I held no regrets.

"Don't make me regret inviting you along."

CHAPTER EIGHT

ARIELLA

I blinked several times over and opened my eyes. My vision swam, and my stomach roiled.

"Good, you're awake."

I opened my mouth to announce that I was going to be sick when Ben brought me over a small trash can with a plastic throwaway shopping bag inside.

Was it that obvious?

I wiped the beads of sweat from my forehead and sat up. The room spun in the process.

I shut my eyes but clutched the small can before I heaved up my lunch from earlier.

What was he doing here?

Where was I? The sun hadn't set yet. What time was it?

Had Jaxson and the others realized I'd gone missing?

"You'll feel better soon," Ben said, his hand on my arm rubbing in soft motions, which made my stomach somersault.

I shrugged away from his touch. "Ben," I rasped, my voice rough, my mouth dry.

I wanted to get up, run away, and get the hell away from my ex-husband. I'd heard he'd been released from prison and that his conviction had been overturned. Apparently, Benjamin hadn't been responsible for stealing millions of dollars along with countless other financial crimes.

I hadn't known he was a kidnapper.

He was full of surprises.

I guess we both were.

It didn't matter to me whether he was guilty or not, I didn't want to be with him, and the fact he drugged me and dragged me to—wherever the hell we were —didn't make me change my mind.

Was I in a hotel room? The bedroom looked strangely familiar. A feeling of déjà vu wafted over me like fog.

Ben was an idiot. If he brought me to a hotel, then he would have had to use a credit card. The Eagle Tactical guys could track him and find me, hopefully before it was too late.

"Good, you're looking more awake already." He grabbed my arm and tied fabric around my wrist, pinning me to the bedpost.

"Ben." My voice hitched in warning as I struggled to keep my left arm away from him. I was still heavily sedated, making it nearly impossible for me to fight back. "Don't do this, please. Let me go."

I doubted I could run, even if I could get to my feet.

He huffed under his breath. "Let you go?" He climbed onto the mattress and straddled my body to keep me from fighting him.

Ben pinned my other arm down and tied me to the opposite bedpost. "I plan to have a little fun with you. After all, isn't that what you did with me? Pretending?"

"What are you talking about?" I shrugged away, trying to escape his putrid breath and his body that towered above mine.

My hands were bound, and while I had the use of my legs, I also was still far too weak to do much. Soon I would be completely at his mercy.

What did he plan to do with me?

Would he kill me?

He sunk his weight against mine, sitting down, pinning me further into the mattress. Ben leaned down, his breath hot against my ear, a knife in his left hand. If he thought he was arousing me, he was dead wrong.

He dragged the blade against my cheek as he drew blood.

I winced but didn't scream.

"You forgot to mention you were C.I.A.." Benjamin pulled back and stared down at me.

I didn't know what to say.

I never thought he'd find out.

"I finally figured out how to make you speechless. It's a real shame I had to learn the truth while I was in prison." He dragged the sharp tip of the blade down my neck and toward my cleavage.

This time he didn't draw blood, only scratched the surface.

My mouth felt like it was filled with cotton balls. I licked my lips. "Can I have some water?" Whatever he'd given me to sedate me had made me thirsty.

Maybe I could trick him into letting me get a drink of water or use the bathroom.

I wanted him off me.

He glanced me over. His eyes narrowed as he stared at me. "I don't think so."

"Please." My voice was soft as I pleaded with him.

He tore my blouse with the blade, leaving me at his mercy.

"Ben, please stop." I trembled from the cool air in the hotel room, my lacy crimson bra on display as he palmed the material. "Ben. Get off me."

"Do you really think you're in charge?" Ben growled.

I flinched but, because of the restraints, was unable to move any farther away. I squirmed to get away but he had a knife and I was bound to the bedposts.

"You want the truth." I stared at him, the sedative wearing off. My wrists hurt where he'd bound them above my head, spread out. "Release me, and I'll tell you everything."

"I didn't drag you here to lie to me!" Ben hopped off my frame and grabbed a clear crystal vase. He threw it across the room, and it shattered against the wall.

I took a slow and even breath. "You're right," I said. "I owe you the truth." At least some semblance of what he believed to be true.

Would it be enough for him to let me go?

I doubted he'd set me free.

As the grogginess faded from my head, I recognized the room. We were in a hotel: Blue Sky Resort if I wasn't mistaken.

I hated that damn place. It seemed like everything bad always happened there, and it wasn't even a crappy motel.

Maybe they needed to hire their own security team.

"I'm waiting," Ben said. He folded his arms across his chest.

My cheek stung but I had to ignore the pain if I wanted to get out of this alive. At least he wasn't throwing anything across the room or at me.

He would when he found out the truth.

CHAPTER NINE

LINCOLN

"Lincoln!" Harper waved to me from across the set as I stood near the front entrance.

I'd been manning the entrance and exit for the past couple of hours since Jaxson rushed off with the sheriff.

I'd done my best to avoid Harper while she filmed the movie shoot.

Busted.

She jogged over. A huge grin lit up her face. "I thought I was supposed to text you when I got off work. Couldn't wait to see me?" Harper asked.

She looked lighter, carefree.

Work actually seemed to put her in a chipper mood, which I didn't mind. It meant she'd be easy to handle tonight, at least in the bodyguard respect. While I may have wanted to handle her in a different manner, that was off the table.

"You look great," I said, trying my best to change the subject.

If she hadn't realized I was with Eagle Tactical, I didn't want her to figure it out right now. After all, I wasn't allowed to tell her I was assigned as her personal bodyguard.

What if she figured it out on her own? I was pretty sure the contract was spelled out. I couldn't divulge it, even then, but I hadn't signed the contract. Jaxson Monroe had done that for the team.

"Thanks," Harper said, her cheeks slightly rosy as she blushed and chewed her bottom lip, glancing away. She tucked a strand of hair behind her ear. "We're actually done shooting for today."

"Good." I knew they were done; our shift technically was supposed to end fifteen minutes ago, but I wasn't leaving until I knew without a doubt that she was safe. "How about we head to dinner, and on the way back, we can swing by and get your car?"

Harper slipped her arm into mine. "That sounds fun. What do you have planned for us? I'm hoping it's somewhere low key. I'm not into the tabloids blowing up my phone or social media with the headline 'Harper lands another hottie.'"

I chuckled. "I don't know. That doesn't sound so bad." I leaned in close, my lips just beside her ear as we walked together toward my truck. "So, you think I'm hot?"

She swallowed and glanced away, quiet for a moment, lost in thought.

Was she thinking about the kidnapping?

She'd seen it earlier, been not only a witness to it but almost his next victim.

Harper hadn't said a word to me about it and while I wanted to ask her directly, I couldn't. Not without her knowing that I was hired by the studio.

I had to tread carefully. I liked her and didn't want to hurt her, either.

"Are you okay?" I asked.

"It's just..." she started and then stalled. Her mouth shut, and her stomach grumbled. Harper pointed at the door to my truck. "How about we grab dinner?"

She avoided talking about what happened.

I wanted to hear it from her, what she felt, how she was coping with it.

My guess was not very well.

Although she had done well on set, maybe I was wrong, and her way of dealing with the attack had been to throw herself into her job.

I knew all about that trick.

I unlocked the door and walked around to open it for her, offering her my hand to help her climb into the passenger seat. Once she was seated and her legs swung over in front of her, I shut the door and hurried around to the driver's side.

"How was your day?" Harper asked.

Avoidance.

Maybe I shouldn't have been quite so shocked that she was focusing on me and keeping the topic far from herself and what she'd witnessed and experienced today.

How would I get her to open up to me without confiding in her about myself?

"Let's see," I said, starting the truck's engine. "I had a nice, hot cup of coffee that no one stole." I glanced at her, and her eyes widened before she burst out laughing.

"Real smooth there, handsome."

I laughed under my breath; she'd caught me off guard with her compliment. "After my hot cup of coffee," I said, finishing my thought, "I relaxed until I was called into work unexpectedly."

Harper exhaled a loud breath. "That's a bummer. Enough about work. Can you take me someplace where we can see the stars? I live in the city, and there's always so much light pollution back home."

"Sure, we can do that after we grab a bite to eat. By then, the sun will have set." I knew just the place to take her that was remote and beautiful.

———

We finished dinner, and I drove up the mountain pass toward my place.

I passed the road for my home and kept heading north to a clearing that I knew would be abandoned.

"You really know how to pick a quiet spot. You don't plan on murdering me up here, right?" Harper joked.

I shut off the engine and stepped out into the darkness, leaving the headlights on for a minute while I grabbed a blanket from the backseat and laid it out to sit on. "Have a seat."

She stalked over to the blanket and sat down.

I killed the lights on the truck and came back in the darkness, having a seat beside her.

"This is nice," she said, lying down on the blanket. She stared up at the night sky, speckled with stars glittering in the distance.

I shifted to lie back down beside her. My knees bent as I stared up at the darkened oblivion. "It is," I said.

I let the silence envelop us, listening instead to the soft breaths that fell from her lips.

Several minutes passed as we stared up above us.

"I thought I might die today," Harper whispered. Her voice was soft but crystal clear.

I reached for her hand.

I wasn't supposed to get close to her. I wasn't supposed to have feelings for the client. I'd met her before we were hired, but did that matter?

I gave her hand a tentative squeeze.

She shifted onto her side and curled up against me.

I pulled her close, protecting and shielding her from the world around us.

"Do you want to talk about it?" I asked. I wasn't going to pry or force her to discuss what happened, but if she wanted to confide in me, I would be there for her.

She chewed her bottom lip, the moonlight casting a soft, blue glow over her features. "I guess you didn't hear about the abduction from the set today. A girl was taken from the parking lot. Apparently, she was with the security team who was hired by the movie studio."

I held my tongue, not wanting to give anything away. Instead, I held her and listened to what she had to say.

"On my way to lunch, I witnessed this guy carrying a girl to his van. It looked strange. It felt wrong. Everything about it, Lincoln. My stomach was in knots. She didn't move. She wasn't awake. For all I know, she's dead. He forced me into the van but I wouldn't go with him."

I couldn't remain quiet any longer. "But you fought him."

"I did," Harper said and nodded adamantly. "I gouged his eyes. I lunged at him and threw myself out of the van. I wanted to help the girl who was lying there, but I couldn't." Her voice cracked.

"You saved yourself, and there is nothing wrong with that," I said and pushed the long strands of her hair out of her face and behind her neck. My fingers danced over her skin. "You were brave, and by escaping, you were able to get help and notify law enforcement about what happened."

She let out a soft breath and rested her head on my shoulder. "Yeah. I never thought about it like that."

"Well, you should. You did good not going with him. Fighting him off probably saved your life."

While I understood who the culprit was, I didn't know what his motives were or if he was capable of murder.

Ben had taken Ariella for a reason, but Harper would have been a loose end.

He would have had no need to keep her alive.

Harper shivered in my arms. "How about we head back?" I suggested. I didn't have a jacket to loan her.

My job was to look out for her, and I was doing a terrible job of that if she was freezing in the forest.

"Just one more minute?" she whispered, her attention not the least bit on the night sky.

Her warm hand rested against my chest, and a moment later, she straddled me, and her mouth covered mine.

CHAPTER TEN

HARPER

I wasn't the kind of girl who kissed on a first date.

Well, technically, this was date number two with Lincoln. Even so, I wasn't even a three-date kind of girl.

I always took things slow.

Which no one ever would have believed, given the tabloid articles and pictures that surfaced.

The girl in those photographs wasn't me. Well, physically, yes, I was the one being photographed, but it wasn't who I was or wanted to become.

It wasn't me.

I'd been young, naive, and deceived.

With Lincoln, everything felt different. My heart pitter-pattered against my chest and soared the moment our lips met.

I leaned in first. I took the initiative, climbing above him.

His hands nestled at my waist. His fingers caressed my lower back, inching my shirt up slightly. The soft pads of his fingertips elicited a response that set my body on fire, wild and alive.

"Harper," he murmured.

I wanted to rock my hips into his, but I still had some semblance of self-control, even if it was only a tiny bit.

It faded fast.

I moaned as we kissed, and my tongue teased his lips apart, desiring further exploration.

I wanted him, and I was pretty sure he wanted me too.

"We can't," he said.

My eyes flashed open, and I pulled back.

Burned.

Why couldn't we? "Are you married?" I was an idiot, believing a nice, good-looking guy like him was still single and available.

"No. I'm not married," he said.

"Engaged?" I wasn't the kind of girl to break up a marriage or an engagement.

Throwing myself at Lincoln had been foolish.

I climbed off him, wrapped my arms around myself, and hurried to his truck.

I sat down in the front seat and waited for him to drive me back to the studio lot where I could pick up my car.

I never wanted to see him again.

He grabbed the blanket outside, folding it before he opened the back door of the truck, and tossed it inside haphazardly.

I yanked on the belt buckle and snapped it into place. Folding my arms across my chest, I stared out the side window, refusing to speak to him.

Lincoln opened the driver's side door, hopped in, but he didn't start the truck. Instead, we sat together in silence.

"I'm not married and I'm not engaged."

I no longer cared what he was or wasn't, for that matter. I shot him a nasty glare. "So, what, you're just not attracted to me? How does that make me feel any better?"

Lincoln let out an enormous sigh.

"What?" I wasn't sure I even wanted to know, but now that he'd made it clear the problem was me, I was livid.

He started the engine. "I'm attracted to you," Lincoln muttered under his breath. "My dick won't shut the hell up."

CHAPTER ELEVEN

JAXSON

The sheriff headed inside the resort first, speaking with the clerk at reception along with the security staff who appeared more like rent a cops than anything else. They were worthless and should have been fired.

Assuming she was in the suite, they were on the first floor, just down the hallway, but the clerk hadn't seen anyone matching either of their descriptions come through the front door.

That didn't mean anything. There were numerous entrances and exits for the resort.

If Ben was here, he wouldn't have waltzed in through the front door bringing an unconscious woman with him. It would have aroused suspicion.

Ben may have been a first-class asshole, but I doubted that he was a complete idiot.

Did he have a plan?

Did he intend to kidnap Ariella, force her to marry him again, or change her mind and win her back?

My stomach somersaulted at the thought of Ben putting his hands anywhere on her.

I'd kill him if he hurt her.

She was mine.

I should have protected her, kept an eye on her. It was no secret Ben had made it known that he was coming to find her. I just didn't have the slightest notion what it had meant.

Guilt swept over me.

I could have stopped this before it ever started.

I should have put a security detail on Ariella.

Though she'd have killed me if she'd have ever found out, it would have been worth her anger toward me, knowing that she'd have been safe.

Officers rushed guests back into their rooms as SWAT barreled down the hotel room door and burst inside.

I followed a few feet behind them, catching sight of Ariella tied up on the bed, her face bruised and cheek bloody. Her shirt was torn, her red, lacy bra exposed.

I untied her hands and she pulled her shirt closed, bunched together in her hands.

SWAT and the accompanying officers cleared the scene.

A broken window beside the bed held a trace of blood.

The curtain blew with the wind.

"He knew you were coming," Ariella whispered, her bottom lip trembling. "It isn't over."

———

Declan picked up Izzie from daycare.

It was late by the time we finished up for the night and headed home.

Ariella had to give her statement to the sheriff, and then we had to get a ride back to the lot to pick up my truck. She handed me the keys, but I kept hers.

I wasn't letting her drive back to the house. We'd drive into work tomorrow if she was up for it.

The sun began to go down beyond the horizon, but it wasn't dark yet.

Ariella remained silent as I drove us home.

Declan's car was parked out front. Skylar still wasn't home, but she was an adult. We'd yet to have a conversation, Skylar and me, about how long she planned on staying. She'd made it clear she wasn't leaving town, but I hadn't given her an open invitation to move in with me, either.

That was a conversation for another day. At this rate, another week.

Other things took priority, like protecting Ariella and finding Ben.

Ariella held an ice pack against her freshly bandaged cheek.

I parked the truck in the driveway and stepped out, coming around to help her out of the car.

She hadn't budged.

Ariella handed me the compress that was now warm. She stepped out, walking alongside me.

I wrapped an arm around her waist, keeping her close, protecting her.

The moment I approached the door, Declan threw it open and greeted us.

"Hey, glad you're all right," Declan said. He stepped aside, granting us entrance inside our home. "I just fed Izzie a snack."

I shut the door and locked it behind us.

Ariella hurried up the stairs without so much as a word.

"Mac and cheese!" Izzie exclaimed from the kitchen table. She hopped down from her booster seat and ran toward the door, sticky fingers and all. "Daddy!" Izzie held her arms into the air for me to pick her up.

I lifted her into my arms, giving her a bear hug.

Izzie scrunched her nose and nuzzled mine as she giggled wildly.

"Are you sure you didn't give her a plate of sugar with that macaroni and cheese?" I asked with a hearty laugh before I planted her feet firmly back on the ground.

My little toddler tore off for the kitchen table to finish her snack, which was more along the lines of dinner, but I wasn't going to argue semantics. I appreciated Declan's help.

"Nah, I just gave her a shot of liquor with her milk," Declan joked.

"Of course, you did." I kicked off my shoes and kept a watchful eye on the stairwell. Ariella hadn't come back downstairs.

Was she avoiding Declan and Izzie, or had she just gone up to take a shower and get cleaned up?

I hadn't heard the water start for the bath.

Declan lowered his voice. "How is she?" he asked, nodding toward the stairs.

"She hasn't said much since we found her at the hotel. The bastard snuck out the window of the first floor. It wasn't too difficult."

"Damn," Declan muttered. "So, he's still at large?"

I exhaled a heavy sigh. "Yes." I'd have to arm the alarm, just in case he decided to show up. I'd have done it the moment I came home, but I suspected Declan would take off soon.

"From what I saw, she looked pretty banged up," Declan said. He slipped on his shoes and grabbed a light jacket that he had brought with him.

I stood by the door, leaning against the material, my arms folded across my chest. "Yeah, he knocked her around pretty good, assaulted her, I'm not sure if anything else happened."

I ran a hand through my hair, frustrated that I hadn't gotten there sooner to protect her.

It was my fault that I hadn't put a detail on her and made sure she was safe from that monster.

"Don't beat yourself up over it," Declan said. "You couldn't have known what he was capable of. Ariella never told you. Right?"

With my lips tight, I glanced up at Declan. That didn't make me feel the least bit better. "Right."

I should have seen it coming.

It was my job to anticipate the unexpected, and it was no surprise that Benjamin Ryan had intended to show up looking for Ariella.

I had thought he'd come to win her back.

"I was going to head out, but maybe you should go and check on Ariella first," Declan said.

If I did that, we might never leave the bedroom. He had no idea that we were more than friends. "You go ahead. I can manage around here."

"Are you sure?" Declan asked.

"Yeah. Thanks for your offer." The last thing I needed was for him to witness something transpiring between the two of us, not that I figured Ariella and I would have sex tonight. But to say that was the last thing on my mind, would have been a lie.

"I'll see you tomorrow." Declan opened the front door and stepped outside.

I watched and waited until he got into his car to shut the door and lock it.

I armed the alarm.

Skylar still wasn't home yet, but she had her own code to shut it off.

"Daddy!" Izzie waved to get my attention, her fingers covered in bright orange goop.

"How about we take you upstairs and get you cleaned up?" I wasn't sure if Ariella was in the bathroom upstairs or not, but at the very least, I could wash up Izzie in the master bath.

"Where's Ariella?" Izzie asked. It was the first time that I'd heard Izzie say her name correctly. She was growing up so fast.

"She's upstairs. Ariella had a busy day today." I didn't want to worry Izzie or scare her. She didn't need to know what Ariella had been through. However, she was likely to have questions once she saw Ariella's bruises and abrasions on her face.

Izzie playfully stomped up the stairs, each step louder than the previous. I shook my head, smiling at how nice it was to be oblivious to the dangers of the outside world.

That wasn't entirely true, though. Izzie had been held hostage with Ariella in my home. It hadn't been a good day, and there had been nightmares that followed, another reason Ariella and I had to be careful about sharing a bed together.

I hated the distance that I'd been forced to put between us, hiding our relationship from Izzie, but how could I explain to my daughter that Ariella wasn't her mother and may never be a mom to her, but was a girl I liked a lot, including intimately? That wasn't a conversation to be held with a three-year-old.

I didn't know what the future held for Ariella and me. The fact we worked together and lived under the same roof complicated matters. More so, Ariella's past complicated matters. She'd lost a son.

Did she even want to be a mother to Izzie full-time?

"Ariella!" Izzie squealed, clomping up the last few steps before running down the hallway. The bathroom door was open, the light off.

I walked past my bedroom, and farther down the hallway was the guest bedroom where Ariella slept. Both doors were shut with no sign of her.

"Come on," I said and lifted Izzie into my arms, zooming her forward like an airplane, making sounds of a propeller with my lips before putting her down on the bathroom rug. I flipped on the light switch, and she stripped down while I ran the bathwater.

I gave Izzie a bath, cleaning the cheesy disaster that had managed to cake on her arms, fingers, and even in her hair.

Afterward, I dried her off, put her into her pajamas, fed her a healthy snack, and then read her a very short story before tucking her into bed. I turned on her nightlight and quietly exited her bedroom, my back to the hallway.

I bumped into Ariella.

"Sorry," she said, quick to apologize.

I reached for her hands as they dangled at her sides. "You have nothing to apologize for. How about we head downstairs and find something to eat?"

"I'm not hungry. I was just going to head to bed."

"You need to eat something. I'll see if I have any soup in the freezer." I led her down the stairs, my hand in hers, not letting her sneak off to bed.

She sat quietly at the table while I heated up some chicken noodle soup. "You really don't have to make that for me. I doubt I can eat much of anything."

I grabbed a soft ice pack from the freezer and wrapped a clean hand towel around it, bringing it up to her cheek.

She winced before I even touched her, and then when she must have realized I wasn't going to hurt her, she eased back.

I dropped a soft kiss on the top of her head before retreating back into the kitchen by the stove to check on dinner. I heated up some leftovers from yesterday because while Ariella may not have been starving, I was famished.

Thirty minutes later, and two bowls of soup eaten, she placed her spoon down.

"Wow, I ate more than I thought I would," she said.

"Good." I cleaned up the dishes and shut off the lights.

Skylar still wasn't home, and I hadn't gotten any texts from her. Maybe she had a boyfriend I didn't know about? "Have you heard from Skylar?" I asked, doubtful that Ariella knew anything more than I did, but they were both girls.

Didn't girls talk?

"No," Ariella said as she followed me to the sofa to sit. "It's not my day to watch her."

"I see you still have your sense of humor." I pulled her into my lap and grabbed the blanket off the back of the sofa, pulling it around us. "Can I do anything for you? Get you anything?"

"No, that feels nice," she whispered, her eyes closing as I wrapped my arms around her protectively.

"That was the point," I whispered into her ear, smiling, relieved that she let me hold her.

Her voice was soft, tentative. "I want to tell you what happened, but you have to promise not to be mad."

I couldn't do that, not if she meant that she didn't want me to be angry with Ben.

He'd drugged her, assaulted her, and who knows what else he'd have done if we hadn't shown up when we did.

"I have no reason to be upset with you." I wanted it made clear that my anger wasn't directed at her. "You didn't do anything wrong, Freckles."

"It's my fault. All of it."

CHAPTER TWELVE

LINCOLN

I drove Harper back to the studio to pick up her car.

Surprisingly, the studio hadn't asked us to keep watch overnight. The stars' trailers were locked up along with the film equipment.

I shut off the engine and climbed out, intending to walk her to her car. I wasn't going to leave her, and I needed to make sure she got back to the motel without any trouble.

After all, I was still her bodyguard while she was out of her motel room.

"You don't have to walk me to my car. Isn't that kind of cliché?" Harper asked.

"It's something a gentleman should always do," I said. I walked alongside her, a couple of short strides to her rental car.

The tension between us had mounted since my confession that she'd managed to turn me on.

She didn't appear disgusted by my remark, and while I'd wanted to hold my tongue, the truth of it was that she needed to hear it.

Harper had gotten the thought stuck inside her head that I wasn't interested in her or wasn't available, neither of which was true.

Approaching her car, I backed her against the door, my hands on her hips. My lips teased her neck, drinking her in, kissing her softly and slowly, wanting her to know that I desired every inch of her.

Her hands slid into my back pants pockets, pulling me closer. "Come inside with me."

"We're not teenagers anymore," I said with a hearty laugh.

She had a small rental car. There was no way it would be comfortable having sex in there, not to mention the fact I was supposed to keep my hands to myself.

I failed miserably.

"I meant my movie trailer. I have the keys. It's just you and me here." Harper rocked her hips against mine. "I like you, Lincoln. I can't say that about too many guys I've known." She leaned in and planted a swift kiss to my lips. "Please don't disappoint me."

How could I say no to her? I wanted her.

She wanted me.

Why did things have to be so damned complicated?

I threaded my fingers into hers. "Lead the way," I whispered.

CHAPTER THIRTEEN

HARPER

I thought he'd turn me down.

I was certain Lincoln would have made some lame excuse and leave me standing alone in the field, kicking up dirt as his truck tore away.

He wasn't like the other guys I'd been with, after only one thing: fame.

I hurried across the lot, my hand latched tight to Lincoln's as I pulled him with me to the studio trailer. I dug out my key and unlocked the door.

His hands were on my hips the entire time, his lips on my neck as he pushed my hair to the side.

"Lincoln," I moaned as he did things to my neck that made my body tremble and grow weak. I struggled to stand, thanks to him.

Glancing over my shoulder at him, I had to take a step back to open the trailer door, bumping up tighter against his body.

I could feel his excitement poking into me, the evidence of his arousal hard and promising of things to come.

With one of his large, firm hands planted on my hip, he guided me back as I opened the door before we fumbled inside, slipping out of our shoes.

I let go of him long enough to cross my arms over my waist and pull my shirt up and over my head, tossing it across the room.

Lincoln followed me, his lips back down against my neck, dipping into my cleavage, his hands at my waist keeping me close and tight as I fell back against the mattress.

He towered above, undoing the buttons on his shirt, taking his sweet time as he stared down at me, pausing for a moment after his shirt was unbuttoned.

"What is it?" I whispered, staring up at him.

Before he could answer me, I sat up and pushed his shirt over his arms. It fell to the floor in a heap.

I undid the button on his dark jeans, unzipping the material, my fingers grazing over his bulge.

Lincoln moaned as I touched him, and he pushed his jeans to the floor. The only remaining piece of fabric was his dark black boxers.

"You have too many clothes on," Lincoln said. His fingers caressed my back, and his mouth landed on mine.

He undid my bra, the material gliding down my arms, and I let the cotton undergarment fall to the floor beside the bed.

"Is that better?" I grinned. My eyes momentarily closed as his lips latched on, taking a taste, bringing me to new heights of pleasure as a wave of euphoria fell over me.

Lincoln's lips remained on my breast while his fingers deftly worked at undoing my pants. "Lift your hips," he instructed, and I did as told. He guided my pants off but left my black satin panties.

Thankfully, I'd packed my sexiest pair when I'd traveled. I never thought I'd be grateful to have brought them with me.

Lincoln was a dream come true, a real-life fantasy. Everything about him screamed sexy. My fingers grazed his chest, my palm rubbed over his bare skin, feeling over his muscles. I didn't want this moment to end.

His warm breath trailed a path of fervent kisses along my inner thigh, up toward my heated core.

I gasped and groaned as he kissed and touched me, discarding the last remaining ounce of clothing. His tongue did wonders, bringing me to new heights, dampness coating me, pulse-pounding, ready for him.

"You're so beautiful," he whispered, teasing me, tasting me, and making my body quiver under his touch.

My fingers clenched at the sheets, bunched into fists as my body responded to his ministrations, his tongue and fingers like magic in a way that I'd never quite experienced before.

There'd been others, but none quite so skilled or devoted in the bedroom. My lips parted, gasping for breath, already on the brink when he grabbed a condom from his wallet, opened the wrapper, and slid it on his length before he climbed back up my body.

I leaned forward, covering his mouth, my tongue pushing its way past his lips, hungry for more as he entered me. I moaned, starved, eager to please him. I bent my legs, drawing him deeper within me, eyes closed.

"Look at me," Lincoln commanded, his breathing heavy and raspy.

I struggled to open my eyes, but I gave him what he wanted. An eager moan fell from my lips. My head tipped back against the pillow, back arched as he filled me with each thrust. I was close, but I wanted him there with me, experiencing it together.

Lincoln grunted, and I clenched onto him, feeling him tinkering near the brink of oblivion.

I wrapped my legs around him, dragging him closer, my arms pulling him tight, needing every thrust as much as the last as I drew near.

He gave me what I needed, my body shuddering and pulsating as my heart pounded wildly against my chest, the sound deafening in my ears.

———

I awoke early the next morning. The light streamed in through the curtains of the trailer.

"I have to go," Lincoln whispered, dropping a soft kiss to my lips.

Moaning in protest, my eyes still shut, I reached out and grabbed his arm. "Don't go."

I didn't want him to run off like the others, never to hear from again.

He brushed a strand of hair behind my ear. "I'll pick you up tonight, after work, for dinner. Maybe we can do something fun?"

"I want to go rafting," I whispered, half-asleep. I'd never been, but I had heard while on set that the crew had plans to go on the river. Some were going tubing, others rafting downstream.

The bed dipped. Lincoln perched himself on the edge of the mattress.

I lazily opened my eyes, staring at him. Had I won? Was he going to stay a little while longer? I patted the bed beside me.

"It'll be too late in the evening to go rafting, but we can make a date of it on Saturday. If you don't already have plans," Lincoln said.

I rolled onto my side, pulling the blankets down slightly so he could get a glimpse of what he was missing by leaving. "Come back to bed," I said. "I'll make it worth your while."

Lincoln leaned down, his lips soft and sweet as he dropped a gentle kiss over my lips. "As much as I'd love to do that, I should get out of here before the crew starts showing up for work."

He was right, and as he pulled back to end the kiss, I groaned in protest. "Fine." I pulled the covers up around myself as I sat up, offering him a faint smile.

While I may have wanted him to stay in bed with me all day, we couldn't do that in the trailer.

Chuckling, he stood, fixing the buttons on his shirt. "I look forward to tonight."

———

After Lincoln left, I climbed in the shower, erasing any evidence that I'd had the most amazing and steamy sex of my life.

I didn't want to admit that my heart soared when I was around him.

Breckenridge was supposed to be temporary.

I had no intention of living in a small town in the middle of nowhere, but the thought of leaving hurt.

What did I have at home?

No one.

My house was nice, but it wasn't enough.

It had only been one night, one fabulous, earth-shattering night, but I couldn't let what happened between us change my plans or my life.

Lincoln wasn't about to upend his life and career because of a girl he just met.

Right?

I dressed quickly into my undergarments and a robe and hustled outside in flip-flops to the makeup trailer to finish getting ready.

I tripped over a stone and failed to catch myself in the process, stubbing my toe and then smacking my knee on the ground.

I grimaced and cursed under my breath.

"Are you okay?" Lincoln asked.

He bent down, offering me a hand to help me stand.

My eyes widened before I pulled back and stood without his assistance. "What are you still doing here?" I glanced over at him, noticing his change of clothes and the badge hung on a lanyard around his neck.

The lanyard in giant letters read *SECURITY*.

"Since when do you work here as security?"

CHAPTER FOURTEEN

LINCOLN

I had rushed home just before the sun came up. I hadn't wanted to leave Harper, but I had to get showered and dressed.

I didn't know if I was expected to work security detail today, but after what had transpired yesterday with Ariella, I didn't want to bother her or Jaxson.

I could come in this morning for my shift, and if I wasn't needed, I'd retire for the afternoon.

After yesterday, I expected that Jaxson would want the extra set of eyes on set to make sure everything went smoothly and everyone was all right.

It would be a long day, especially since I was still Harper's bodyguard, but that didn't feel like work.

Spending time with her, was something I wanted to do.

After showering and changing quickly at home, I grabbed a cup of coffee at the local shop, saying hello to Skylar. She scribbled her number on my coffee cup and told me that she hoped I'd call her.

I couldn't tell her I was dating Harper Madison.

Were we even dating?

What happened when the film shoot was complete, and Harper went back to sunny California?

Breckenridge was my life. I loved it here, the quiet solitude.

Los Angeles was nothing like our small town, a little piece of heaven.

Pulling up in the lot, I drove past a dark metallic blue sports car.

I parked my truck and stepped out, walking over toward the car, having a look at it from the outside.

"Can I help you?" a gentleman with a thick Italian accent asked. He was slightly rotund, with a sharp nose and a thick head of dark hair. It had to be dyed. It was almost too black for his age.

The parking lot was still mostly empty. I was early, but Eagle Tactical was expected to arrive on set before the entire cast and crew.

I pulled out my badge. The lanyard had the giant letters *SECURITY* along with my picture on the identification card.

"I'm with security. Can I help you?" I asked, turning the question on him.

He hadn't trespassed yet.

"No," he said. He shook his head and stalked toward his car. "I was just leaving."

———

I'd seen a photograph of Benjamin Ryan.

The mysterious man with the sports car wasn't Ben. I wasn't sure who he was, but I kept a close eye on Harper.

Harper had taken a pretty good fall, tripping over a rock and scraping her knee.

She'd barely been out of her trailer and certainly wasn't dressed for production.

Is that where she was heading when she fell?

"Let me help you," I said, ignoring her question about me being part of the security team for the film production. I didn't offer her just my hand.

Instead, I bent down and reached for her elbow as I helped her to her feet. She could scream at me all she wanted, but I doubted she would do it and make a scene.

She had a reputation to protect, and I suspected that she didn't want anyone to know that we'd slept together.

Though she did have a reputation, according to the studio and the tabloids, the truth was I didn't care what anyone else thought.

I'd spent time with her and gotten to know the real Harper Madison, and she wasn't like anything everyone claimed.

I'd heard the rumors. I chose to ignore them.

Her eyes tightened, and she pulled back. "I don't need your help," she said.

Harper stood and dusted her hands and knees off, the skin on her knee scraped with a small trace of blood that needed to be cleaned up but wouldn't require stitches.

"How about I take you to your trailer and find a first-aid kit?"

She snorted and stepped back. "Leave me alone."

I held up my hands in surrender. "I'm just trying to help."

"I don't want your help."

That was obvious. I held my tongue. There was no point in arguing with her when she was already mad at me. I knew it wouldn't go over well if she found out that I was her bodyguard.

Did she realize that I'd been hired to keep an eye on her off-set, or was she just mad that I was part of the Eagle Tactical team and ran security for the production?

Shit.

Did it matter?

She probably never wanted to see me again, and I had to keep an eye on her tonight. If I couldn't do it, I could ask Jaxson or one of the other guys, but she'd know they were hired as her bodyguard, and I doubted she'd be on board with the company.

Harper blew past me for her trailer.

I needed to give her space. If she wanted to be left alone, it wasn't my job to hover over her and help. I may have tried to protect her, clean up her skinned knee, and hug her, but she wasn't a little kid.

I had to respect that she probably wanted nothing to do with me.

Jaxson strolled over, his hands buried in his jacket. He nodded at me while glancing at Harper's trailer.

"Everything okay?"

"Couldn't be better. How's Ariella doing?" I asked. I hadn't seen her this morning and wanted desperately to talk about anything else. The least I could do was ask about her after what she'd been through yesterday.

His eyes narrowed, staring at me. He could probably see right through my facade, but he didn't say anything further about Harper. "She's recovering," Jaxson said. "I suggested she speak to a therapist but you know Ariella. She's tough and likes to think she can handle everything on her own."

"She's been through a lot," I said. That wasn't a bad idea, her seeking counseling. "Talking with someone could definitely help. And her ex-husband, Ben? Was he caught?"

I had hoped they had put the bastard behind bars.

"There's been no sign of him. Police have an A.P.B. out, but the sheriff hasn't reached out. He's out there, somewhere." Jaxson's brow furrowed.

"The police will find him."

"Yeah," Jaxson answered gruffly.

"What about Mason? How's he doing?" I asked.

"Mason's back in the office. The doctor told him he could do desk work for the next two weeks until he goes back again for another checkup."

It was good to hear that Mason was doing better. It was pretty tough to see what he'd been through and losing his uncle couldn't have been easy, either.

"Excuse me!" a young woman with strawberry-blonde hair rushed over to us.

"Yes, how can we help you?" I asked, glancing down at her badge, making sure that she belonged on the production set.

Her cheeks were pale, her eyes wide. "I can't find Harper Madison anywhere. The star of the movie, she's gone."

"She's in her trailer," I said, walking alongside the young blonde toward Harper's trailer, where things had been hot and steamy the night before.

I didn't enter.

I gave a firm, forceful knock.

"Ms. Madison," I said, not wanting anyone to know about the relationship between us.

There was no answer.

She was probably avoiding me.

Jaxson followed behind us. "Harper Madison. This is security," Jaxson said.

I stepped aside, and he gave another firm knock on the trailer door that was shut. "We're coming inside," he announced, opening the door.

It had been left unlocked, and Jaxson stepped inside first.

I followed behind, glancing around, but Harper was nowhere to be found. "Maybe she's on set or in makeup or hair," I suggested to the young woman.

"No. I'm the makeup artist, and she's late."

"How late?" I asked. I knocked on the bathroom door of the trailer and checked to find it empty. I didn't see her car keys or cell phone, but I wasn't sure that meant anything. I'd have to check the lot to see if her car was where she'd left it last night.

"Over an hour," the young woman said.

"I'm sure she hasn't gone far. Why don't you head back to your trailer, and we'll find her?" I said.

She retreated from the trailer, and I glanced at Jaxson, waiting until we were alone.

"What is it?" Jaxson asked.

"Harper was pissed when she found out that I'm working security for the film." I glanced out the back window of the trailer, over the sink, which led to the parking lot. There were too many vehicles to notice whether her car had been moved or not.

Jaxson's jaw was tight, his body stiff. "You think she fled?"

I didn't know her well enough to determine how she dealt with stress, or anger, for that matter. "Maybe. I hope that's all it is. There was a guy outside this morning in the parking lot with his Lotus Evora. A luxury car like that stands out."

"No kidding. I don't think I've ever seen one in Montana, let alone Breckenridge," Jaxson said. "Could it have been a studio executive?"

Anything was possible, but I didn't get that vibe when I looked at him. "That would be a relief if that's all it was, in which case, wouldn't he still be here?"

I headed out of the trailer and walked around past the ropes put up to the parking lot.

There was no sign of Harper's rental car or the luxurious sports car that I'd seen earlier. I pulled out my cell phone and dialed Mason. Since he was at the office, I asked him to track Harper's cell phone and call me back or text me her location.

A few minutes later, my phone buzzed with a text. "I know where she is," I said, glancing at Jaxson.

"How far away?" His expression was grim.

Pretty soon, other people would start noticing Harper wasn't on set too. She wasn't that far away, but she was near the river and appeared to be near an entry point with rafts available to the public for rent.

If she rented a raft and didn't have experience, I didn't want to think about what might happen to her.

It was spring thaw, which meant the river was high and the rapids dangerous.

CHAPTER FIFTEEN

HARPER

How dare he!

I stormed across the plowed field for my car and high-tailed it out of the lot. I rolled down the windows and belted out a scream, my hands gripping the steering wheel in tight fists.

"What a jerk!" I couldn't believe he tricked me into thinking he had shown up on set last night for me.

Is that all I'd been to him, just another assignment?

I hit the gas hard. My foot pressed tight on the pedal as I headed for the dusty mountain road.

I'd heard the stream last night when we'd been camping out under the stars. While I wanted nothing to do with Lincoln, the thought of rafting felt good, taking control, with no one else around for miles, in solitude.

The only problem was where the hell was I going to get a raft?

I raced up the mountain before I eventually pulled over on a gravel road and dug out my cell phone.

I had shitty service in the woods, and the internet was slow, but it worked.

I pulled up rental facilities and clicked on the information for a nearby location, letting GPS lead me where I needed to go.

Twenty minutes later, I had parked the car, paid for a rental raft, foregoing the opportunity to ride with a guide.

The attendant on duty went on and on about the danger of the river and his recommendation on hiring a guide.

It wasn't that I couldn't afford a guide, I preferred to be alone. Apparently, he had trouble grasping that fact.

Finally, he handed me the paperwork and I signed the legal waiver with a lot of jargon about injuries and death that I didn't bother to read thoroughly.

"Be sure to grab a helmet and life vest outside. Those items are hanging just on the other side of that wall."

"Thanks."

I headed outside, showed my receipt to the attendant on duty, and was handed a small raft, made to comfortably hold two guests, along with a paddle.

"Make sure you grab a helmet and vest," the gentleman said.

I pretended not to hear him. I carried the raft and placed it at the edge of the launch pad, a cement pathway that led to the river on a steep decline. I didn't see any boats, and the river was quiet, at least in terms of rentals.

It was, after all, a Tuesday morning, and I was probably their first customer for the day.

"Harper!" Lincoln's voice carried with the wind as I regrettably glanced back toward the voice.

He slammed the truck door shut and came jogging in my direction.

Oh hell, no.

He wasn't going to talk me out of this.

I pushed the raft farther into the water, my feet and knees getting wet as I made sure to push away from the cement. The last thing I wanted was for Lincoln to follow me.

I jumped onto the raft and used the paddle to hurry away from the river's edge. I didn't get far.

Lincoln chased after me, forging into the water, splashing, and then launching his body entirely in as he began swimming over toward me.

"Everything okay, ma'am?" the attendant shouted toward me.

I rolled my eyes at Lincoln. He wasn't going to hurt me, just annoy the hell out of me. "Yes, my boyfriend is just an idiot!" I shouted back at the gentleman.

Lincoln surfaced, his arms at the edge of the raft, holding on. I couldn't see the bottom of the river.

Was it deep?

"Boyfriend, huh?"

"Don't flatter yourself. I figured if I called you the guy I regrettably slept with, he might phone the cops. Do you want to climb on?" He'd probably do it without my permission, seeing as how he'd chased me downstream.

"I thought you'd never ask," Lincoln said. He hoisted himself onto the raft.

The boat swayed.

My eyes widened, and I pushed myself to the opposite side to keep the raft from tipping. "Careful!" I warned.

"Funny, I should be telling you that. No helmet. No life vest. And one paddle."

He knew just what to say, to get under my skin.

"Well, I wasn't expecting company."

"There's another rental unit a few miles downstream. We can grab the rest of the necessary gear as long as we're going rafting." Lincoln gestured at the paddle. "It's all yours."

"Gee, thanks. You're quite the gentleman, aren't you?" I mocked while attempting to paddle.

I couldn't reach both sides from where I sat.

We needed another paddle.

Lincoln grinned the entire time, pleased with the predicament.

I wanted to hate him, but that huge grin and his carefree attitude just made me almost relax.

"Are you having fun?" I still gave him hell. It was the least I could do considering what he put me through, not telling me the truth.

Had he ever intended on mentioning to me that he worked security for the production?

Did he think I wouldn't notice?

"I am, but I think it would be helpful if we carefully changed positions. I'll ride your back, and you take the lead."

I raised an eyebrow at his suggestion.

"The longer you stare at me with that come-hither look, the longer we'll be sitting on the river barely moving."

"It's not a come-hither look," I retorted.

We hadn't hit rapids yet, and I couldn't even see or hear them in the distance.

Slow and careful, we switched positions as I scooted around to the front center, and Lincoln sat behind me. "Of course, it's not," Lincoln said with a sly grin.

Thankfully, I was seated in front. At least he couldn't see the expression on my face.

We sat in silence for several minutes as I paddled from one side to the other, keeping us moving downstream in mostly the center. I avoided the rocks to the right and the tree root to the left of the riverbank.

The raft shifted slightly, and Lincoln's warm hands brushed the hair to the side of my neck.

With one hand, I gripped the raft and with the other, the handle of the paddle. "What are you doing?" I squeaked.

I hadn't intended to sound quite so unsure and not the least bit confident, but he'd caught me off-guard.

"Apologizing," his husky voice whispered into my ear, sending a shiver down my spine.

No way.

That wasn't going to cut it. "Sex isn't an apology," I said and glanced at him over my shoulder.

I contemplated smacking him upside the head with my paddle, but I didn't want to knock him overboard or risk him drowning.

The water was dark and deep.

I couldn't see the bottom.

Silence filled the void, and Lincoln pointed up ahead at the ramp and nearby rental station. It looked identical to the previous one that I'd just visited. "Pull up along the ramp," Lincoln said.

Yeah, I'd do that and drop his ass off.

"Sure." I paddled harder, wanting to get there quickly so I could dump him behind.

Lincoln jumped off, his feet getting wet. Not that it mattered. He was still pretty soaked from his earlier swim.

I waited by the entrance as he headed up the platform. The minute his feet were on solid ground, and he faced away from me to grab the gear, I paddled out.

It was a good two minutes before he turned around and noticed. "Harper!"

Snickering, I waved and gave him a salute before paddling downstream.

CHAPTER SIXTEEN

ARIELLA

The film had taken a pause. Without the lead actress, there wasn't much that could be done.

That was fine with me. I wasn't in the mood to work.

I wanted to curl up on the sofa with a carton of mint chocolate chip and eat away my feelings.

Jaxson stalked over toward me. He'd been watching me all day.

Mostly, I was grateful for the concern, but sometimes I just wanted my space too.

"I just got a text from Lincoln. He found Harper, and she's heading downriver," Jaxson said.

I didn't understand what he meant. "Downriver?" I hadn't lived in Breckenridge that long. I'd survived the winter, that was about it. Did we need to intervene? "Should we head out there and help?"

It didn't appear that filming would resume anytime soon.

"I think Lincoln's got this one handled. Harper's gone rafting, and he's the best guide I know," Jaxson said.

"Oh." That sounded kind of fun. "Maybe we should do that sometime? The three of us?" I suggested.

"The three of us," Jaxson repeated slowly. Was he trying to figure out who the third person I invited along with us? It wasn't Lincoln.

"Yes, it'd be nice to do something with you and Izzie." I liked spending time with them.

Was that a bad idea?

Did Jaxson have commitment issues?

We hadn't exactly told anyone about our relationship.

I wasn't looking for another husband. One had been enough, but I did want more with Jaxson.

He wasn't just a fling.

"You're quiet," Jaxson said.

"Just thinking."

"Uh oh," he teased and nudged me. "That can't be good."

I rolled my eyes and grabbed his arms, pinning them behind his back, my body pressed tight against his. I leaned up on my tiptoes to reach his ears. "Any chance you have handcuffs around here."

I needed to forget, to push the fear that crept in at night and held me hostage.

Jaxson raised an eyebrow. "Maybe, but they wouldn't be for me, Freckles."

I gulped and stared up into his calm blue eyes. He caught me off guard. I never expected him to admit that he had handcuffs. What else did he have or was it strictly for business' sake? He was former military and he worked security, but I'd never so much as seen his metal cuffs.

"You're blushing," Jaxson whispered into my ear.

My grip on his wrists wasn't that strong, and he broke free.

Grabbing my wrists, he spun me around, my hands pinned at my back, his body pressed against mine. With one hand, he held me tight, and with the other, he brushed the hair to one side of my neck, his breath caressing my skin.

"Have you ever used handcuffs in the bedroom?" he asked.

I glanced around, grateful no one paid either of us any attention.

"Have you?" I countered. A hint of nervousness struck my voice. Had he noticed?

He pulled me closer and around the corner on the opposite side of the trailer where we were out of sight of the handful of crew members who had stuck around. Most had left, and the director, twenty minutes earlier, had called it a wrap for the day.

"Are you okay?" he asked.

We were off the clock, but we hadn't left.

Jaxson insisted that we wait until we were the last to remain.

Like we were actually working and doing our jobs.

Someone could have driven off with one of the stars' trailers, and neither of us would have noticed.

I tipped my head upward, leaning in but not quite kissing him yet, letting the moment linger between us.

"I'm worried about you, Freckles."

I leaned into his touch, wrapping my arms around his neck, embracing him. He had no idea how much such a simple gesture had soothed me. "Me too," I whispered.

His breath tickled my neck as he spoke in a whisper. "I've been waiting to tell you this, but I made reservations for the spa. You and Hazel can spend the entire day tomorrow relaxing."

Visiting a spa sounded wonderful. "Hazel is coming with me?" That was a pleasant surprise.

"Yes, Hazel and Mason are getting under each other's skin, so we thought it would be a good idea to send the girls somewhere for a treat."

"Get us out of your hair?" I joked, laughing under my breath. "What about work?"

It was the middle of the week. I couldn't just blow off my job, even if Jaxson was my boss.

He leaned closer, his lips grazing my ear, and it sent a shudder down my spine.

Just being in his proximity, made my insides warm and toasty.

"I'm sure you can make it up to me in other ways," Jaxson said.

"If it involves handcuffs, then I'm the one securing you to the bed." While the thought just days ago would have been fun, being bold and adventurous, I wasn't ready to let my guard down after what happened with Ben at the hotel.

Smirking, he shook his head. "We'll see."

His hands caressed my waist as he tugged me closer.

I rested my hands on his chest, our bodies practically sandwiched together. While it wasn't particularly cool out, the slight chill of the wind was long forgotten, with his body heat warming me all over.

"I want you to spend the day unwinding, Freckles. You deserve it." He dropped a soft kiss to my cheek, and my eyelids fluttered shut.

I shifted slightly, leaning up on my tiptoes to taste his lips, wanting reassurances that whatever happened, we'd get through this together.

"I'm scared," I whispered, the words difficult to voice aloud.

I opened my eyes, feeling his steady gaze on me.

"I know," Jaxson said. "I won't let him touch you ever again."

It wasn't just the fact that Benjamin was still out there, waiting to make his move.

There was so much that I hadn't told Jaxson and when I did, would he ever look at me the same way again? I had intended to tell him last night, but I hadn't found the confidence, too afraid to come clean.

"I need to tell you something." My hands trembled against his chest, and I gripped his shirt, balling my hands into fists.

I leaned in, stealing another kiss, another taste, afraid that it might very well be the last.

CHAPTER SEVENTEEN

LINCOLN

That little spitfire!

Harper had snuck away the moment I had my back turned and been distracted.

She had no idea the danger of the rapids up ahead, especially this time of year.

A few cars were parked at the loading dock, but the one that stood out to me was the same one I'd seen earlier that morning, a shiny metallic blue Lotus. There was no way there were two of those vehicles in Breckenridge.

I exhaled a heavy breath.

Shit.

Where the hell was the Italian-looking guy who had driven the car? He wasn't outside.

Had he gone downriver already?

Would Harper run into him?

I hurried inside the small shop, but there was still no sign of him. "Busy morning?" I asked, trying to make small talk while fishing for information.

"Same as usual," the man behind the counter said. He spoke slowly, his movements not the least bit quick.

I yanked out my wallet. It was soaked along with my phone. Just great. "I'd like to rent a raft for one, please. Also, do you have any rope I can purchase?" I pulled out my credit card, not wanting to waste a beat.

The gentleman behind the counter leisurely strolled across the room to retrieve the rope. "Do you need six feet or twelve?"

"Six is fine." I didn't need a lot.

If I'd have had cash on me, it would have made the transaction a lot quicker. The moment he was nearly finished and handed me the receipt, I scribbled my signature and hurried out of the complex.

"Don't forget your helmet and life jacket."

I didn't let him finish his sentence. I'd heard it all before and knew the items were stored outside.

This wasn't my first rafting trip and hopefully wouldn't be my last. I hurried to the attendant and showed him my receipt.

While he grabbed the raft, I secured a helmet, the life jacket, and grabbed an extra set for Harper. She'd wear them before we hit the rapids.

I may not have felt I needed them, familiar with the river, but I wanted her to wear them. If I wasn't doing what I was asking her to do, she'd never listen to me.

I dropped the rope, helmet, and life jacket into the raft and launched the craft into the river.

The cool water felt good on my feet, and I climbed on, getting myself situated before I began paddling with a good hustle.

I needed to catch up to Harper.

I hurried downstream. At least I was moving in the same direction as the current.

The river forked up ahead, and I needed to get to her before she veered off in the wrong direction.

Eventually, the river came back together, but to the right held rougher rapids. For a novice, it was better to take the left side.

Did I need to worry about the mysterious man I'd spotted earlier that morning?

Was he out for a water adventure on the river or did he have something else in mind?

Had he known where Harper was or what she'd been doing?

I'd been able to track her with Mason's help. It hadn't been tough pinging her cell phone to the nearest tower, and then zeroing in on her location.

Had the Italian man done the same?

What did he want with Harper?

He didn't look like the type of guy who would be into water sports or go anywhere near a river.

I paddled hard and fast.

In the distance, I caught a glance at her raft. The fork was up ahead, and she headed toward the right.

Shit.

"Harper!" I shouted, hoping that she'd listen to my advice.

Her long blonde hair darted around as she glanced over her shoulder at me.

I paddled harder and faster, closing the gap between us. I honestly thought she'd try to outrun me. Instead, she put her paddle down in the raft and waited for me to approach.

My heart raced as I caught up to her, and as I came alongside her raft, I grabbed the rope and tied our rafts together at the handles.

A weak smile played on her lips. "I didn't think you'd follow me after I left your ass twice," Harper said.

"I'm persistent."

Harper laughed and shook her head. "You're something else."

Grinning, I secured a knot, keeping our rafts together. I handed her a helmet. "Put this on."

"And if I don't?"

"I won't let you go down the rougher rapids." The rafts were already nearing the right entrance of the fork, and it would take too much time to get to the opposite side. "Please."

She huffed under her breath and took the helmet from my hands, securing it on her head and clipping it under her chin.

I reached behind me for the life jacket. "This too, please."

At least I didn't have to hold her down and force her to wear it. I didn't think that would have gone over too well.

She'd have likely thrown me into the water.

"Fine. I can't afford to die out here. Too much paperwork for you, right?"

I swallowed the lump in my throat.

Had she known that I was hired as her bodyguard?

Did she realize the job went beyond just running security detail on set?

If she hadn't figured it out already, I couldn't risk her discovering the truth.

Already, she was pissed, but she'd hate me.

"It was a joke. Relax," Harper said. She secured the life jacket and reached for her paddle. "Are you going to untie us now?"

A huge grin crossed my face. There was no chance in hell that I was untying our rafts until I was confident that she was done for the day. She'd have to be out of the raft and on dry land. "You'd like that, wouldn't you?"

Her fingers grazed over the knot that I'd tied. She studied it for a long moment before giving up.

I wasn't sure whether she thought she couldn't untie it or just didn't care that much.

Maybe she didn't mind being stuck with me?

I had all day to convince her that she wasn't just an assignment.

The raft picked up speed as the current grew faster the closer we approached the rapids.

We'd been chatting and laughing, and I'd nearly missed the fact that we were drawing nearer to the rough waters ahead.

CHAPTER EIGHTEEN

JAXSON

Whatever Ariella wanted to tell me, it couldn't be that big of a deal. I knew she was former C.I.A., and not even her husband at the time had known about her job.

She had told me once that while he may not have been guilty of the financial crimes that he'd been convicted of, he certainly wasn't innocent, either.

I hadn't known what she'd meant until she'd been drugged and dragged by the monster into his van and held captive. Thankfully, we'd found her before he could have done any further damage or harm to her, but she was different.

Every time I reached out to touch her, embrace her, show her that I was there for her, I could feel her hesitate.

Maybe she didn't even realize that she was doing it, but I noticed.

"How about we have this conversation somewhere a little more private?" I suggested. "You want to take a walk?" If she was ready to talk about Ben, her ex-husband, then I was ready to listen.

Whether I could remain calm, was another obstacle that I'd have to face.

Her hand slid into mine as we walked alongside one another, away from the set toward the edge of the forest in the distance.

"I just—I don't want you to hate me when you hear the truth."

I could never hate her. I might be disappointed, but hate was a strong word.

"Let me guess. You married Benjamin because the C.I.A. advised you to do so?" I wasn't sure that was what she had intended to tell me, but it was a stab in the dark.

How far off was I?

"Not quite," Ariella said. Her hand fell from mine, and she folded her arms across her chest.

I stayed close, our bodies almost touching at our hips as we walked alongside one another.

I waited for her to elaborate, to tell me what had her so tied up in a knot that even Ben had managed to get to her.

"My ex-husband, Ben," she reiterated, "I didn't meet him by chance or by accident."

"You were staking him out," I said.

Her brow furrowed. "It wasn't like I was a field agent and was meant to go undercover. I was out having drinks with my team from the C.I.A., and while we were investigating Benjamin Ryan at the office, we ran into him at the bar. He kept staring at me and eventually came over and asked me to dance. It was obvious he liked me and wanted to get to know me."

"Bold." I shouldn't have been surprised by his move, considering what he'd done just yesterday.

"Yeah, I was hesitant, but turning him down, I was more afraid of what it might mean to the investigation. So, I danced with him, had a drink, and then he gave me his number. He told me the next move was mine."

That surprised me. I hadn't thought she'd have been the type to have willingly thrown herself into a burning building.

"I know what you're thinking, I did this to myself, but my boss insisted I call Ben."

My hands bunched into fists. I'd kill whoever her boss had been if I ran into him. "I never thought that, Freckles."

This wasn't in any way her fault. Even if she had made a poor choice in dating him, clearly, there had been something worth searching out.

She'd married him. It hadn't all been because of her boss. She must have loved him at one time.

Ariella started walking again, this time along the edge of the forest, as we reached the end of the open field. "Ben had been a gentleman, and the investigation hadn't turned up anything, so when he asked me out a second time, part of me wanted to see him again."

"But?" I had the sneaking suspicion that someone, namely her boss, pushed her toward Ben.

"But my boss insisted that if Benjamin Ryan wasn't involved in the human trafficking ring, then it had to be one of his colleagues or his friends, and they were shuttling women through the building where he lived."

My stomach sank at the thought of the danger that lurked. "Could it have just been a neighbor? Did Ben have an apartment or a condo someplace in New York?" I asked.

"That was what I thought, he lived in an apartment, but his phone records indicated his involvement. It turns out his brother, Richard, was living with him. He'd been in and out of prison and had friends over when I went back to his place after a few months of dating."

"What happened?" Clearly, she was still alive, relatively unharmed. Hell, she'd gone on to marry the guy.

Ariella shrugged her shoulders. "Nothing." She stopped walking and turned back toward the production set.

The trailers in the distance were small, and it was too difficult to see if everyone had left for the day or if any stragglers remained. Most had cleared out when we'd started our walk.

"You never told your supervisor?" I asked. I found that hard to believe. She didn't seem the type to betray the C.I.A. in favor of a man.

"I reported it, and his brother was arrested, but since Ben didn't seem to be involved and at the time I stupidly liked him, we continued dating. Honestly, a small part of me was relieved it was his brother, and the C.I.A. had been tracking the wrong guy. After the place was raided, Benjamin moved out, and all of it stayed behind. His brother, the drama, the investigation, it was in the past. As far as I knew, Ben and Richard never spoke again, and I never told Ben that I was the reason his brother went back to prison."

I took her hand in mine. "That was probably for the best. It wouldn't have gone over well and could have put your life in more danger."

"Yes, so instead, I married him. Grand idea," she quipped.

"We all make mistakes. We're allowed one really bad one," I teased.

She squeezed my hand. "Thanks. Ben hadn't realized I was with the C.I.A. until he was in prison. Someone told him. I have no idea if it was Richard or someone else. That's why he came here, and he blames me for all of it."

I pulled her tight into my arms, embracing her. "None of this is your fault."

Did she know that?

"We'll find Ben, and until he's located, you'll have one of the Eagle Tactical team watching your six."

"You're giving me a bodyguard?" Ariella smiled, laughing under her breath. "I should have expected that from you, but I did not see that coming."

"Well, you should have," I said.

For the most part, I planned on being her bodyguard and protector, but if I couldn't be around, then it would be one of the other guys I served with, men who had my back.

"Does that mean you'll be joining our lady's day tomorrow at the spa?" Her hands slipped under the back of my shirt, her fingers caressing my skin.

I wanted to be the one to give her a massage. Maybe we could do that tonight. Just the two of us? "How about I give you a little preview of your spa day at home?"

She pulled back slightly, her arms still wrapped around my waist as she stared up at me. "Hmmm," she said, mulling it over. "Will that massage lead to something else even more pleasurable because as tired as I am, I could get on board with that arrangement."

Leaning in, I dropped tender, featherlight kisses across her neck. "I wouldn't want to keep you awake."

"Oh, it would be worth it," Ariella said. One hand stayed pressed to my lower back, her other threaded through my hair.

Her touch felt wonderful, relaxing, hypnotic. I pulled her closer, growling into her ear. "Maybe we should take you home, get you undressed and ready for tomorrow's spa day."

I had other plans in mind that involved a full body massage and listening to her sweet moans and gasps as she pleaded for more.

CHAPTER NINETEEN

ARIELLA

The studio was pissed that Harper left for the day and filming was halted, but there wasn't anything we could do about it.

I headed home, and Jaxson stayed on my tail the entire time.

He planned to pick Izzie up before dinner but was letting her spend a little longer with her friends.

He was right. It was good for Izzie to have others to play with who were her age. She had no siblings, and I wasn't sure I could go through conceiving a child again. I'd lost my son, and to this day, it still haunted me.

I had worked through the grief, but seeing Ben had brought all those emotions and more, with memories resurfacing.

He hadn't always been the bad guy. At one time, I had loved him, but it felt like a lifetime ago.

Finally home, I sunk into the mattress, my head against the pillow, eyes closed, naked.

Jaxson's warmth and weight nestled against my hips, pressing me down farther into the bedsheets.

He lathered lotion on his hands, rubbing his palms together to warm his hands before he caressed my shoulders and down my back.

A soft sigh escaped past my lips.

Jaxson's hands were strong and firm, and his movements lulled me more toward slumber than anything else.

I had expected him to take the opportunity with the two of us alone to seduce me, but he surprised me. His hands massaged down my back in a soft, soothing motion.

My body drifted further toward slumber, relaxed and without a thought or care in the world.

His touch had a healing effect.

Jaxson lifted his hips off mine, and I moaned in protest.

"Do you want me to keep going?" he asked. His breath was soft and warm as he leaned closer, planting a kiss on my neck.

"Yes." It took every amount of measurable strength to answer him.

His lips were warm and soft against my skin. "Sleep, Freckles."

I opened my mouth to protest, but it took too much energy to answer.

His hands continued massaging over my bare skin as I drifted to sleep.

———

I had fallen asleep from the most amazing massage of my life. Jaxson had worked his magic, and it hadn't been remotely sexual like I had expected.

After dinner, we curled up on the sofa and watched a movie together once Izzie was tucked into bed.

Skylar staggered in well past midnight, but neither of us said anything to her. She was a grown adult, but it was clear that she'd been out partying.

Jaxson gave me the day off, and Hazel was supposed to drop by in the morning at the house. We planned to grab breakfast together and then head to the spa.

I needed a day away from the world, a chance to unwind and not think about what happened with Ben.

The massage last night had lulled me into a peaceful slumber, free of nightmares.

While awake, I constantly glanced over my shoulder, waiting for Ben to reappear.

What I wouldn't give to feel calm and safe.

Jaxson was right.

I needed to speak with someone about it and maybe a therapist would help? As I exhaled a heavy sigh, a loud thud echoed outside.

My heart leaped and I jumped. I hurried to the window and glanced outside. I expected to see a car and had hoped Hazel was early.

No one was there.

My hands trembled.

I double checked to make sure the alarm was armed.

It wasn't Ben. He didn't know where I lived or how to find me. Even if he'd tracked me down to Breckenridge, there was no way he knew that I lived with Jaxson.

He shouldn't have even known we were an item and he hadn't mentioned it while I'd been held captive just a few days ago.

Maybe living with Jaxson indefinitely wasn't such a bad idea. With Jaxson, I felt safe and protected.

The truth was that I was afraid, fearful that if I spoke with a therapist, she'd try to convince me to move out, that a relationship with my boss was a terrible idea.

CHAPTER TWENTY

HARPER

I needed coffee, something strong with an extra jolt of caffeine. I'd spent last night at the shitty motel, alone. Lincoln and I had grabbed dinner and drinks at the nearby bar after we finished rafting.

He may have been hot, but he'd lied to me.

Lincoln worked security for the production set along with his buddies.

Maybe I shouldn't have been angry, but why hadn't he told me?

Had he known who I was when we had first stumbled into each other at the coffee shop?

Here I was again, in dire need of a shot of caffeine. On my way to the set, I stopped at the local coffee shop where I'd first run into Lincoln.

What were the odds I'd see him again today?

Probably pretty good, but that was when I got to the set. Thankfully, this morning he wasn't there.

I breathed a sigh of relief and headed straight to the register to give my order to the girl behind the counter. Her name tag read *Skylar*.

It was the same girl who had butchered my name the last time.

Wonderful.

"Harper?" An unfamiliar voice stepped up behind me in the line to order.

Finishing my order, I slid my credit card into the chip reader before glancing over my shoulder. "Yes?"

I didn't recognize the gentleman with short, military-cropped hair and wire-rimmed glasses. He wore blue jeans and a dress shirt and barely looked out of high school. "Charles Stone, I'm with the Hollywood Chronicle."

He pulled his lanyard with his PRESS credentials out of his jeans pocket.

Inwardly, I groaned.

"Do you have a minute?" he asked.

Behind him, the shop door opened and Lincoln headed inside.

Could this day get any worse?

"Are you stalking me?" I shot at Lincoln before returning my attention to the news reporter.

He wasn't a local.

The Hollywood Chronicle was an entertainment magazine based out of Los Angeles, which meant Lincoln wouldn't have recognized him. "Yes, join me, Charles. I'll grab us a table," I said a little too loudly, for Lincoln to hear.

I snatched my coffee from the counter and hurried to sit down.

Charles skipped the line and grabbed a chair.

Smart man.

He probably was worried I'd change my mind.

I also was on a time crunch, which he seemed to recognize. I sat across from Charles at the round table, one leg propped over the other, staring past him at Lincoln.

Lincoln scowled as he ordered, every so often, glancing back in my direction.

Was he jealous? I didn't want to make eye contact with him. I shifted my chair, hoping I could ignore him. Pretty soon, he'd have his coffee and leave, right?

No such luck.

He stood by the counter, waiting for his drink, watching me the entire time.

"Boyfriend?" Charles asked, glancing over his shoulder.

"Just someone from the set," I said and gestured for him to continue. "What would you like to know?"

Charles pulled out his phone. "Do you mind if I record our conversation?"

"Go ahead."

He opened an app and recorded an audio stream. "Thank you." He appeared young, perhaps bright, but also like I was his first assignment. "You're a long way from Hollywood," I said, surprised he'd chased me down in Breckenridge.

Charles laughed under his breath. "Yeah." He started his questions, asking me about the film, if I enjoyed the small town and what my dream role would be.

I kept my voice down to make sure it didn't carry throughout the coffee shop. Other than Charles and Lincoln, no one else here knew who I was. At least no one else had paid me any special attention. It was nice to be a nobody. I couldn't remember ever having that before.

"And one last question," Charles said, "do you mind if we take a photograph or two outside? I'd love to have a picture to go along with the article."

"How about you come to the set, and during lunch I'll give you that photo?"

I didn't want him snapping pictures of me without my hair and makeup done. I didn't look my best, and the last thing I wanted was to be interviewed in a

Hollywood magazine looking like I'd just rolled out of bed, which was pretty much what I'd done.

I sipped the last of my coffee and stood, walking over and dumping the empty cup into the trash. I pushed open the glass door and headed outside.

Charles followed after me, phone in hand. "It's just one picture. We can always touch it up later," Charles said.

He lifted his phone and began snapping photos, ignoring my request.

I held my hand up in front of my face.

Asshole.

I'd been naïve to think that he'd actually do what I'd asked. He was probably one of the jerks who had staked out my hotel the first night that I'd been in town.

"I said no!"

"The lady asked you to leave her alone," Lincoln's gruff voice answered. His heavy footfalls clomped from behind.

I didn't need him to fight my battles, but he was quite a lot bigger and taller than Charles. Lincoln was every bit of a man.

"Fine!" Charles shoved his phone into his pocket. "I'm leaving. Already got the shot that I wanted anyhow."

Lincoln snarled at the man and stomped closer. "Give me your phone."

"No." Charles's bottom lip trembled.

Lincoln towered above Charles and grabbed him by the lapels of his shirt. "I wasn't asking."

———

I didn't have time to deal with Charles or Lincoln, for that matter. Already, I was running late, and after bailing yesterday, I needed to get to the set.

I hurried to my car, leaving the two of them to battle it out in the parking lot. I didn't think Lincoln would actually assault the idiot with the Hollywood Chronicle, but if he did, I wasn't going to intervene.

Hightailing it out of the parking lot, I made a sharp left and hurried toward the set.

My foot was lead on the gas, and as I rounded a bend in the road, a car was stopped on the main drag.

I slammed my foot on the brake, but it took too long. I plowed into the small four-door sedan.

Metal crunched on metal.

Shit.

CHAPTER TWENTY-ONE

ARIELLA

I felt like a stupid teenager, glancing out the window shades, waiting for Hazel to show up.

We weren't best friends, but I didn't know too many people in town, and small towns weren't easy for making friends, especially in winter.

Although winter was thankfully behind us, it didn't make it any easier to meet new people when I spent most of my days working and evenings with Jaxson and Izzie. I held no regrets.

Jaxson had already left for the day to go to the set of the film production. While I wanted him to play hooky with us, someone had to be the responsible one.

A pickup truck entered the driveway and pulled up out front of the house. Mason was behind the wheel.

Hazel climbed out and gave a wave before sauntering up to the front door.

I shut off the alarm and swung open the door before she had time to knock. "Are you ready?" I tried to hide the enthusiasm from my voice, but I was failing at it miserably.

"Yes, but it's taken me all morning to convince Mason not to follow us to the spa. He made me promise that I would call him when we check-in and again when we leave," Hazel said.

I'd have thought he was overprotective if it wasn't for the fact we'd both been kidnapped and taken against our will too many times recently. "Jaxson made me promise the same thing, plus he's tracking my phone."

"Oh, my gosh!" Hazel squealed. She threw her arms around me, greeting me with a proper hello.

Mason turned the truck around and headed out of the driveway and back down the mountain.

"Are you ready for a girls' day?" I armed the alarm and shut the door, locking it behind myself.

Hazel hurried to my car and waited by the passenger side door. It was clear she was as excited as I was to get out and have some fun.

In a matter of minutes, we were on our way. I sat behind the wheel, talking animatedly with Hazel. "You have to tell me everything about what's been going on in your life."

We'd been texting each other on occasion, but there was so much to catch up on. She had moved in with Mason after he'd been shot, and we hadn't spent any time alone to chat about what that had been like.

"My life has been surrounded by Mason, and that's it," Hazel said. "Imagine caring for Jaxson twenty-four-seven."

That didn't sound so terrible. "That much fun." She didn't sound like she had enjoyed it.

Mason was a handsome guy, and while I hadn't exactly gotten off on the right foot with him, it seemed the two of them shared a history together.

"Well, playing nurse, in the beginning, was fun, especially when he had me dress up in a sexy costume," Hazel said.

I glanced at her and caught her blushing as she stared out the window. "And?" I turned off the mountain pass and headed across the main road toward the spa.

"It's kind of hard to do anything when he's on bed rest and not allowed to engage in fun activities. It was torture playing nurse, not being able to do the things I wanted to do to him."

Giggling, I bit my bottom lip. "That isn't the case anymore, though. Right?" It had been weeks since he'd been shot, and the doctor had cleared him for desk duty.

"Well, we've had to take it slow," Hazel said. "I mean, I'm sure he wants to do more, and so do I, but he has needed time to heal."

"I understand."

"Do you? I know you think that you and Jaxson are a secret, but it's a really obvious secret. Like everyone in Breckenridge probably knows," Hazel said.

I gripped the steering wheel harder. "Please tell me you're joking."

Hazel stared at me as I focused on the road. "Am I wrong? Are you seriously telling me that the two of you are just friends?"

A deer leaped across the road, and I slammed on my brakes to keep from plowing into the creature.

The seatbelt locked in place from the abrupt stop.

Seconds later, we were thrown forward, metal ground together, as someone ran into us.

My heart hammered in my chest. "Are you okay?" I asked.

"Yeah."

I glanced in the rearview mirror. "Harper?" I whispered, unlocking the door.

I unbuckled my seatbelt and stepped out, surprised to see that she'd been the one who rammed into my car.

Hazel stepped out of the passenger side too. "Are you okay?" Hazel asked.

"Yeah, I'm fine." Just a bit shaken up, but relieved it was only Harper.

My first fear had been that Ben had found me.

Was that irrational? He was out there, somewhere.

Would I always be looking over my shoulder?

There were no recent hotel or other credit card receipts to determine where he'd gone, no cell phone that we'd found and been able to track.

"I'm so sorry," Harper apologized. "I didn't see your car stopped around the bend."

A pickup truck slowed on its approach.

"Seriously?" Hazel muttered under her breath.

Was she grumbling about Harper hitting us or the approaching driver?

CHAPTER TWENTY-TWO

HARPER

"I'm sorry," I apologized again. "I didn't see you stopped. We can just exchange insurance and be on our way."

I stepped closer, getting a better look at the two young women I'd rear-ended. "You're the girl from the film set. The one who was taken."

I would never forget that moment.

It was forever ingrained in my mind.

The brunette exhaled a heavy sigh. "I should probably thank you for trying to stop Ben."

I hadn't succeeded, but at least she was alive. "I'm glad you're okay," I said.

She was all right, wasn't she?

She had a bandage on her cheek but otherwise looked all right.

A pickup truck slowed and pulled over behind us.

The two girls didn't look flustered, just angry. Was it because I hit their car? It was an accident. "Again, I'm sorry. I'll pay for the damage."

"Is everyone okay?" a gruff voice asked, his window rolled down.

"We're fine, Mason," Ariella said. "I can't believe you're following us!"

I reached into my pocket for my phone.

Did I need to call for help? Would Lincoln come if I called him?

"How about I give Hazel, Ariella, and you a lift? I can drop the girls off at the spa and drive you wherever you need to go." Mason said. "Pull your car over to the side of the road, and I'll give Declan's shop a call to get the cars towed and repaired."

Mine was a rental. "That isn't necessary." I didn't know this guy. The two girls did, but I wasn't climbing into his truck.

"Fine," Ariella grumbled. She moved her car and tossed Mason her car keys. The back of her vehicle had buckled from impact and had taken the brunt of the damage compared to my rental.

"Are you sure it's safe?" I asked, whispering my question to Ariella.

She was one of the security teams for the production set. If she trusted going with him, then it was okay.

Right?

"He's my boyfriend," Hazel said. "He'll take you wherever you need to go in town."

"You should come with us to the spa," Ariella said.

Gosh, that sounded perfect. However, I had a production to shoot. I couldn't bail two days in a row, even if I had been in a car accident. It didn't help that the crash had been my fault.

"I can't," I said.

"How about you come by after you're finished filming?" Ariella asked. "We have a girls' night in tonight."

"With wine!" Hazel added. It was clear she was excited and probably needed a break from whatever she did for a living.

Hell, I needed one too.

"You should come," Hazel said.

That sounded amazing. "Just the girls?" I'd miss spending the evening with Lincoln, but he was just a fling.

Wasn't he?

Besides, he had lied about working security on set. Some time apart wasn't a bad idea.

In a few short days, I'd be finished filming and back in Los Angeles.

"Yes," Ariella said. "I'll text you the information if you don't mind giving me your phone number."

———

I didn't want to admit the jealousy that seeped through my veins as Mason dropped me off at the set.

The director didn't look thrilled that I was late, again. He stormed toward me, and before he could blast me with being irresponsible or not caring about the role, I offered up an apology.

"I'm sorry," I said, quick to apologize on my way to makeup.

I didn't stop to make small talk or even offer up an excuse.

"Where the hell is your bodyguard?" the director fumed, stomping behind me.

I swallowed the lump buried in my throat. "Bodyguard?" I repeated.

My voice was hoarse. He'd caught me off-guard.

"I have a bodyguard?"

Is that why Lincoln had insisted on jumping into the damned river to go rafting with me? Even after I'd left him at the dock, he'd rented a raft and caught up with me.

I'd been fooled into thinking that he'd wanted to spend time with me.

That I'd meant something to him!

Tears threatened my vision.

The director scoffed under his breath. "Of course, you have someone watching your every move. Do you honestly believe the studio trusted you after the last incident when you worked for me?"

The sun beat down, and the air felt hot, suffocating.

"You don't know anything about me." I hurried into the makeup trailer and slammed the door shut behind myself, locking it.

The young woman, Melissa, sat on the bed. Her attention had been on her phone when I burst through the door. "Sorry I'm late. I rear-ended a car on my way in this morning."

Her eyes widened, and she stood. "Are you okay?" Her eyes raked over me.

Did I not look okay? "Fine, just a little off today."

It was hard not to be flustered from it, along with the argument from the director which didn't even take into account what I'd heard about Lincoln.

He was my bodyguard, wasn't he?

I'd seen him on set and off. Almost every night, he'd been with me since the moment that I had arrived in town.

Had that been planned?

My instincts told me to run, but without a car, I had no way of leaving. I slumped into the chair in front of the mirror, a scowl etched to my face as Melissa towered from above.

"Any chance I can borrow your car?"

CHAPTER TWENTY-THREE

LINCOLN

I'd snatched the bastard's phone and smashed it into a thousand tiny pieces on the ground before leaving the coffee shop.

How dare he take pictures of Harper when she explicitly asked him not to do so and even had invited him onto the set.

What a creep!

The twat had made me lose sight of Harper. I was supposed to keep an eye on her, even from a distance, but I had neglected to do that. Showing up at the coffee shop just moments behind her hadn't been a coincidence.

My phone had been set with an alarm to alert me when she'd been on the move.

I hurried toward the set, slowing the truck down, when I noticed her car and Ariella's both banged up on the side of the road.

I slammed my hand against the steering wheel. "Shit."

Where was she now?

Using my vehicle's hands-free device, I phoned Jaxson.

"Everything okay? Where are you?" Jaxson asked.

"Running late. Harper seems to have trouble follow her. I had to deal with a reporter, and I'm almost at the set, but I noticed two cars on the side of the road, and one of them was Harper's," I said. I didn't further elaborate, not wanting to worry Jaxson.

Had Ariella called him?

Where had the girls gone? Did a stranger pick them up?

"Harper just showed up a few minutes ago. The director seems pretty pissed. I should warn you. He let it slip about the studio hiring a bodyguard for her."

Why the hell had the director gone and done that? Was it to make my life miserable?

"Wonderful," I muttered under my breath. There was little chance Harper was going to let me spend the evening with her and keep an eye on her.

I wasn't concerned about her alone at the hotel. It was what trouble she might land herself in while on her own.

She had never just been an assignment. I wanted to spend time with her.

By now, word had begun to spread about a Hollywood starlet and film crew in the valley. The last thing I needed was Harper to have more press hounding her.

"Ariella called me on the way to the spa. She invited Harper over for a girls' night tonight."

Interesting. Since when had Harper made friends with Ariella? I hadn't seen them together except for the two cars abandoned on the side of the road. "Did Ariella mention anything about her car?"

"Yeah, Harper plowed into her when the girls stopped short from hitting a deer that ran across the road," Jaxson said.

He didn't seem angry with Harper about the accident. "Was everyone okay?"

I pulled into the parking lot of the production set and shut off the truck. I grabbed my phone as it switched from the speakers back to my cell phone.

"Just a little shaken up. Ariella and Hazel went to the spa as planned. Mason gave all of them a ride."

Climbing out of the truck, I breathed a sigh of relief. At least it wasn't Ben who had snatched the girls or forced them to go with him. Most of the town's folk were friendly and would happily offer a lift, but there were a few people who had once lived off-grid who would have worried me.

The majority of those folks had died a few months ago in an ambush. There were a few people who mysteriously survived. Those were the guys who I worried about, the ones who had gotten away unscathed.

I slung my credentials around my neck. The lanyard swung as I strolled toward the set at a quickened pace. While I hadn't intended on being late, it wasn't in good form.

Catching sight of Jaxson, we ended the call, and I shoved my phone into my pocket. I kept an eye on Harper's trailer. I doubted she was in there. She was probably with hair and makeup or wardrobe getting ready.

From across the lawn a few strides away, the director had his phone plastered to his ear as he pounded on one of the trailers.

"You can kiss your career goodbye!" the director shouted.

The trailer door swung open, and Harper stomped down the steps.

Jaxson and I exchanged glances. We'd been hired to protect Harper and keep the set free from bystanders. But she didn't seem like she needed looking after right now.

She could take care of herself.

"Really?" she snorted and stormed up to face him. While she was shorter, she didn't look the least bit intimidated by him. "Maybe I should call your wife, tell her how you coerced me into taking nudes so I'd get my first lead role and then proceeded to share them with the tabloids?"

The director's face turned bright red. "You wanted to take those photographs."

"The hell I did!" Harper shouted. She didn't seem to care who heard her or what was said.

I waited for steam to shoot out of the director's ears. "When the studio fires you, don't come crawling back to me to help your career."

He stormed off and threw his clipboard onto the grass like a child having a temper tantrum.

Her hands balled into fists.

She turned on her heels and landed her gaze on me.

Shit.

CHAPTER TWENTY-FOUR

HARPER

The director was a grade-A asshole.

I'd dealt with him one too many times, and today I wasn't in the mood to button my lips and walk on eggshells.

Someone else could do that for him.

I didn't care if I got axed from the gig. It was a crummy acting job for a film that probably would have tanked anyway.

Lincoln watched me from across the set.

Had he seen the outburst between the director and me?

Great.

I ran a hand through my hair, not giving a crap about the production anymore. The director had stormed off, and I wasn't in the mood to put on a happy face and pretend to be someone I'm not.

Some days I could fall into the role, but after the accident this morning, my world felt upside down.

It didn't help to hear that Lincoln had been hired by the studio as my personal bodyguard.

He didn't hesitate in the slightest. Lincoln approached me, closing the distance between us.

How much had he heard from the director? I pinched the bridge of my nose. If he was here to give me a lecture on acting professional or some other crap, I wasn't in the mood.

"Are you all right?" Lincoln asked, his voice soft and calm yet firm.

"No." Nothing felt all right.

My world spun wildly out of control and while I may have been reckless and stupid yesterday, running off set during filming, today was a new day. I had vowed to take the job seriously and respect the time of the cast and crew.

Little good that had done.

The truth was I wanted to run, but I didn't have a car. It was on the side of the road. Maybe I should have driven it to the set. At least I would have had a vehicle to get around in still. However, I wasn't sure if it was safe to drive. The front end had quite a bit of damage.

The remaining cast members and crew began to pack up for the day, again. With the director gone, it meant another day without shooting.

"Want me to take you somewhere?" Lincoln asked.

Another security guard approached the two of us. "Everything all right?" he asked.

I glanced at his name badge: *Jaxson*. "You're Ariella's husband, right?"

He looked taken aback by the question. "I'm not her husband. We're just friends. Colleagues."

"Oh, my apologizes." I had thought they were together when she had called him while in Mason's truck and mentioned that he wasn't going to be home tonight during girls' night.

I was mistaken. "I misunderstood. Can you give me a lift to the spa where the girls are? I could use a me day."

I didn't want Lincoln to drive me anywhere and Melissa hadn't been willing to part with the keys to her car. Not that I blamed her, I wouldn't have given me the keys either after I'd smashed my rental.

Jaxson glanced at Lincoln before nodding. "Yes, of course. Follow me."

"Thank you." I left Lincoln standing there as I hurried out to the parking lot with Jaxson.

It wasn't that I didn't trust Lincoln, I did, but I was also seething inside for what he'd done.

He'd lied to me. He had every opportunity yesterday while we were rafting, or even the previous day, to come clean.

No, instead, he'd kept his dirty little secret.

"Everything okay?" Jaxson asked. He unlocked his truck, and I stepped around to the passenger side while he climbed in behind the wheel.

"Just peachy."

He laughed under his breath. "Gosh, you sound like my daughter."

"You have a kid?" Was Ariella the mother? That made sense, why they might have lived together.

He smiled, tightlipped, not answering my question. He seemed protective of his daughter. That wasn't such a bad trait.

Sighing, I glanced back at the studio as Jaxson pulled out of the parking lot. There was no sign of Lincoln. "Hey, can I ask you something?"

"Shoot," Jaxson said.

Had it been a coincidence that Lincoln had found me at the coffee shop earlier that morning? "If you had to find someone and track them down, how do you go about doing it?"

Jaxson turned the radio down and shifted in the driver's seat.

He glanced at me, eyebrow raised. He didn't answer my question.

"Hypothetically?"

Silence filled the truck.

"If you're wondering how Lincoln knew you were at the river, we traced your cell phone location."

It hadn't even occurred to me to ditch my phone.

I wouldn't make that same mistake.

———

I headed into the spa and made a reservation for a massage. I had twenty minutes until my appointment.

Glancing at my watch, I dug my phone out of my pocket and tossed it into the nearby trash. "Track me now," I muttered to myself.

Lincoln knew where I was, but he wouldn't know when I left or where I went afterward.

I doubted the production would continue. With the director pissed and threatening to contact the studio, I would be fired by morning.

I refused to grovel or beg for his forgiveness. He was the reason the studio forced a bodyguard on me, insisting that I couldn't be trusted. I didn't need protection. I wasn't helpless or a damsel in distress, damnit!

While I'd made mistakes and done things that I shouldn't have, on those rare occasions, I'd been drugged or coerced.

The sins of the past followed me like a shadow that I was unable to escape.

"Harper?"

"Ariella?" Hazel stood beside her. "I thought you both had spa appointments?" Were they done already?

"Our appointments got pushed back when we ran late this morning. They were really nice, giving us a later time. What are you doing here?" Ariella asked. "Did you decide to join us for a girls' day?"

I definitely needed to unwind. "Yes, you could say that."

"Do you want me to try to book us all together?" Ariella asked.

"Sure." I could use the company and a friendly face. "Thanks."

Ariella hurried to the receptionist and explained how the three of us were friends and asked if there was anything that could be done to put us all together for our appointments.

———

Every inch of my body ached.

The car accident had been to blame, and while it was entirely my fault, it didn't make everything hurt any less.

A blissful ninety minutes of a hottie giving me a full body massage had been quite a treat.

As angry as I was at Lincoln, the heat had dissipated, and I felt much more relaxed.

We all got facials after our full body massages and then manicures and pedicures.

While the morning had started off as a bust, at least the afternoon was definitely getting better. We finished at the spa, and Hazel called Mason to give us a lift back to Ariella's place.

Hazel shoved her phone into her pocket. "He'll be a little while. He's with Jaxson grabbing lunch. They suggested we grab a bite to eat too."

"Is there any place we can eat around here?" I asked. I wasn't familiar with the town.

"Follow us. We know this town inside and out," Ariella said.

They led me to a small café next door. The place seemed crowded for the middle of the week. We waited a few minutes to be seated and were escorted to a table.

Conversations around us clashed together, the noise in the restaurant rising with each other's voices. While it was difficult to hear Ariella and Hazel, it wasn't particularly hard to hear the gentleman one table over, situated behind me.

It seemed the restaurant had added an extra table and chairs to accommodate us, but leaving us very little room of our own.

"I'll offer you double your asking price," the gentleman said. He had an Italian accent, and I tried not to glance over my back to him. I felt like I was in his lap.

"And why would you do that, Enzo?" another male voice asked.

Enzo? I recognized that name.

No.

It couldn't be. I held my breath and refused to turn around to see if it was true.

Enzo Ricci.

The girls read over their menus. I pretended to be interested in mine as I listened to the conversation going on behind me. It was impossible not to hear whatever deal was being made between them.

Could Ariella and Hazel hear it too?

They didn't seem interested. Maybe they were too far away. The restaurant was loud and rather chaotic.

"I prefer to buy out my competition as opposed to other methods," Enzo said.

I swallowed the lump in my throat. The voice no longer just familiar, but I was certain that it was Enzo Ricci, my husband.

CHAPTER TWENTY-FIVE

ARIELLA

Harper held her menu up, oblivious to the fact that I'd tried getting her attention. The restaurant was crowded and busy, but she seemed distracted.

"I don't think she hears you," Hazel said.

I put my menu down, waiting for Harper to glance up.

She didn't budge in the slightest.

Our table was sandwiched into the café, giving very little elbow room, let alone space for privacy.

While I couldn't make out any distinct conversations, I noticed Jayden sitting at the table just behind Harper.

I hadn't met him firsthand, but I knew of him. Everyone in Breckenridge by now knew he was one of the few surviving off-gridders.

How had he survived the massacre from the Russian mob when they'd blown in and slaughtered everyone?

I didn't recognize the gentleman Jayden was with. I couldn't recall ever seeing him before in town. The mysterious man wore an expensive suit and was sharply dressed, obviously well off.

It stood out, with Jayden in his dark black jeans and a white t-shirt that hugged his chest. He was tall but not taller than the mysterious man who sat across from him.

"Harper," I said, trying again to steal away her attention from the menu.

She lowered the menu, her eyes wide, filled with trepidation.

"What is it?" I asked.

Had she forgotten her wallet or something? She looked terrified.

"I need to—" Harper stood and didn't finish her sentence. She grabbed her purse off her chair and high-tailed it out of the restaurant.

"Bathroom?" I guessed, glancing at Hazel. Maybe she could decrypt what I had missed. Where else had she gone off to?

Hazel sipped her glass of water. "You go check on her. I'll wait here."

"Thanks." I stood and hurried after Harper, trying to figure out what happened.

What had I missed?

Maybe she wasn't feeling well. I followed her into the bathroom.

Harper stood hovering over the sink, her hands on either side of the porcelain. The color had drained from her face.

"What's going on?" I asked.

"I heard his voice."

"Whose?" I asked, taking a step closer. I rested a hand on her back. Her body trembled.

"Enzo, my husband."

Shit.

Since when was she married? I ran a hand through my hair, surprised by the news. "You're married?" My voice squeaked, betraying me. Lincoln would be even more shocked than I was, and not happy about it.

I'd never heard about her marrying anyone, but then again, I did not read the tabloids or check out the gossip columns in the entertainment papers. I had heard of Harper Madison before her arrival in Breckenridge.

"I met him in Vegas during a film shoot. He was romantic, charming, and I got really drunk. The rest is a blur, except that I woke up the next morning with his enormous diamond ring on my finger," Harper said.

"What did you do?"

"I ran. A few months ago, I saw a segment on television about the mafia and organized crime across America. Enzo was featured with his buddies, the same guys who had liquored me up that night."

"Shit," I cursed under my breath. The bathroom door swung open, and I froze, worried that Enzo might storm in and join us.

He didn't.

It was one of the waitresses. She headed for a stall.

Breathing a sigh of relief, I waited until the main door swung shut to speak. "We'll get through this. Mason is on the way. He won't let anything happen to you. Did Enzo see you?" It couldn't be a coincidence that he'd shown up in Breckenridge.

Harper rubbed her forehead and splashed cold water on her face. "No, I don't think so."

"That's good," I said. "I can head back to the table, get the check, and have Hazel meet us outside."

The waitress stepped out from the stall. "Are you okay?" she asked. "Do you need me to help?"

"I think we're okay," Harper said, offering a faint smile.

I texted Hazel to meet us outside, that we'd have to grab something to eat later, and then Mason to hurry, that we had a problem.

Hopefully, he'd make it before Enzo spotted us.

I stepped out of the bathroom first, making sure no one was waiting outside to snatch Harper. I had no idea whether Enzo was violent or not.

Had he come to Breckenridge to claim his wife and bring her home with him?

"Come on." I led her through the hallway and made a sharp right heading out of the restaurant. I glanced back toward the table, but it was too hard to see if Hazel had left already or if Enzo was still seated with Jayden.

What did Enzo and Jayden have in common? Why were they having lunch together?

We hurried out through the main exit and stood outside, catching up with Hazel.

"What's going on?" Hazel asked. "Are you okay?" Her attention was entirely on Harper.

Harper wrapped her arms around herself. "I just ran into someone who shouldn't be here."

She didn't elaborate.

Was she worried that if she told Hazel, Lincoln would eventually find out? I couldn't keep it a secret. It was too big, and Harper was in danger.

Wasn't she?

Mason pulled the truck up out front and unlocked the doors. "Are you guys okay?"

"We are now," Harper said. She yanked the back door open and hopped into the back seat. I climbed in beside her.

Were we seriously not going to talk about Enzo and the fact she'd married him? If it had been a moment of regret that she didn't remember, there were ways to fix it.

Divorce was the first option that crossed my mind.

What was she afraid of?

CHAPTER TWENTY-SIX

HARPER

Mason drove us to Ariella's house on the mountain.

I glanced every so often behind us, making sure that Enzo hadn't followed us.

Would he be waiting outside my hotel room tonight when I went home?

How long could I avoid him?

"Is anyone going to tell me why I had to rush over?" Mason asked.

"I don't know," Hazel said. She glanced out the side window. "Maybe Ariella or Harper can answer you."

"Thanks for that," Ariella huffed under her breath. "We saw someone we didn't want to converse with and thought it would be a good idea to leave."

Hazel shifted around in the front seat to face us. "Before we even ordered lunch? You're keeping secrets from me, and I don't like it."

Mason glanced up in the rearview mirror. His gaze landed on me. If I told him, wouldn't he tell all his buddies, and it would get back to Lincoln?

No, thank you.

"You're going to have to tell him," Ariella said. She nudged me with her elbow. "You can trust Mason."

"Right? So, he can go back and tell Lincoln?" I exhaled a loud sigh and folded my arms across my chest. "That's the last thing I need right now, more drama."

I wasn't talking to Lincoln right now. I'd just gotten over the fact that he worked security detail for the set, and today I'd discovered that he had been my bodyguard.

To say I was pissed at him, was an understatement. I couldn't even look at him without boiling over.

Had every night that we'd spent together, under the stars or shacked up in my trailer, been because of his job?

Ariella's voice was soft and quiet as she spoke. "Enzo is here for a reason."

I knew that. It was why my stomach was in knots, and I wanted nothing more than to go home.

I'd trashed my cell phone. I had no idea if the studio had contacted me to fire me.

Maybe I could lie low, hide out with Ariella for a few days, and just let this shit storm that brewed pass over.

Mason cleared his throat. "Does Enzo have a last name?" He didn't even pretend that he couldn't hear what was said between us.

"No." My jaw firm, I refused to give it up. If I did, then he'd find out the truth, that I was married to Enzo.

Mason pulled the vehicle up to the front of the house and turned off the engine. He climbed out with us, walking up to the front door.

Was he just making sure that we got inside, or was he planning on staying?

We followed up to the porch, and Ariella dug out her key. She unlocked the door and let us inside while she disarmed the alarm. "It's girls' night, which means you need to leave," Ariella said, pushing Mason out the door.

He took several strides backward but remained on the porch. "Set the alarm and don't answer the door for anyone," Mason said.

"Relax. Jaxson will be home late tonight. I promise not to let anything happen to your girlfriend," Ariella teased.

"Bye!" Hazel blew him a kiss and waved, giggling. "Shut the door!"

Ariella slammed the front door and armed the alarm.

I stood by the window, watching Mason retreat to his truck. "Is he really leaving?" I asked.

"He'd better," Hazel said, flipping on the lights, making herself at home. "Where's the wine?"

———————

"How's Bear?" Ariella asked.

"Super cute and cuddly," Hazel said. "She's the dog we adopted from Mason's uncle when he died. She is honestly the cutest. I can't see how she doesn't like people. I swear all she does is lick me or cuddle me."

"Sounds like Mason," Ariella giggled, taking another sip of wine.

"Shut it!" Hazel's eyes narrowed as she glared at Ariella.

"What about you?" Ariella turned her attention to me.

"No pets," I said, answering a little too quickly, hoping the conversation was more along the lines of animals than boyfriends.

Hazel tilted her head back, finishing her glass of red wine. She grabbed the bottle and refilled her glass. "Anyone else?"

"I'm good." I didn't need a headache later or to be hungover. I was still on edge after spotting Enzo at the restaurant.

"Fill my glass," Ariella said, wiggling her glass in front of the wine bottle.

"You have to hold it still or I'll make a mess," Hazel said. "I can't pour into a glass that's all over the place."

"That's my tremor."

"No, it's you being drunk," Hazel said with a snort. "Nice try."

"Hey, I walk straighter when I'm drunk," Ariella retorted.

Hazel shook her head and rolled her eyes. "Do you see what I deal with?" She turned her attention back to Ariella. "No, you don't walk straighter when you're drunk. You just don't realize that you're falling over. It's quite amusing."

I sipped my drink, taking in the banter between the two of them. "How long have you two known each other?" I asked.

It seemed like they'd been friends forever.

"Not that long," Hazel answered. "We became friends through work." She lifted the glass to her lips.

Was she avoiding the question? I wasn't quite sure.

"We should toilet paper the neighbor's house!" Ariella squealed. Her eyes were wide and filled with excitement.

That sounded like a terrible idea. "We aren't supposed to leave the house," I said. Why did I get stuck being the responsible person?

"It's dark. What's going to happen in the dark?" Ariella giggled. She finished her glass. I'd only counted two. She mustn't have consumed alcohol very often, or she was a complete lightweight.

"Only murders and kidnappings," Hazel said with a straight face before she burst out laughing. She finished her second glass and poured a third. "Gosh, I need to get laid."

"What?" Ariella spun around on her heels. "Do you mean to tell me that you and Mason haven't done anything—"

Hazel stammered to the front door, pushed the curtains aside as she glanced outside. "I wanted to. You don't know how hard it is to play nurse and not do sexy things with Mason, but he had to heal, and doctor's orders were no sex. Too bad I was only a nurse and couldn't override the doctor's advice."

"Girl, what are you doing with us tonight?" I asked. "It's clear he wants you. I see you want him. Go to him, or since you don't have a car, call him."

"Yes, call him and have phone sex with him," Ariella said, giggling and clapping her hands.

"Oh my gosh! You two are troublemakers," Hazel muttered. She covered her face with her hands.

My stomach grumbled. "I'm hungry. We should order a pizza. Give me your phone." My purse sat at my feet, but I'd already tossed my phone. The decision was spontaneous and not without regret right now.

Hazel dropped her hand into her lap. "Why? You'll just call Mason and embarrass me."

"I won't, I swear." I saluted her.

"I think you're supposed to link pinkies," Ariella said. "Or you could just use my phone." She dug her smartphone out of her pocket. "Here."

Ariella unlocked her phone and handed it to me. "Any recommendations on where to call?" I asked. I didn't know any local pizza places.

After we narrowed down the restaurant and the type of pizza we wanted, I made the call and offered up my credit card to pay. I handed the phone back to Ariella to give the address.

Not even twenty minutes later, there was a firm knock at the door.

"That was quick!" I leaped up and hurried to answer the door.

Ariella shut off the alarm while I unlocked the door without so much as looking out the window or through the peephole which happened to be much too high for me.

A tall, burly gentleman with the same eyes and hair as Enzo towered above me. Time felt as though it stood still. A flash of recognition crossed my gaze. I pushed the door closed, but he shoved his foot inside and thrust it open hard, which forced me to stumble backward.

He flashed a glimpse of his gun holstered to him. "Don't touch that alarm," the stranger said with a thick Italian accent. "Back away slowly. Go, sit on the sofa with the other girl."

Ariella didn't turn around. She slowly shuffled back toward the couch, but never turned her back on him.

How did he find me? "Did Enzo send you?" I asked.

Why else was he here?

"You're coming with me," he said with a dark, sinister laugh.

He wanted me. I didn't need to put their lives in jeopardy.

He tilted his head, staring at me with his eyes of steel. "Isn't it awful running away from your husband? Enzo can take care of you, protect you."

"I'm not his wife," I scoffed at his notion of marriage. "We were in Vegas, and I was drunk, thanks to you and your buddies."

Had they drugged me too? The whole night was a blur.

Ariella stepped between the thug and me. "She's not going with you." She stood her ground. "You need to leave."

He backhanded Ariella across the face. "No one speaks to me in that tone," he growled. His top lip snarled, and the thug leaned in and grabbed Ariella's shirt. He yanked her close and held her tight. "A pretty girl like you, I'll bet you'd sell real quick."

Ariella slammed her fist upward into his jaw.

His eyes flinched, the only evidence of her assault on him. "Is that how you treat guests?" he asked. He unclenched his fist, letting Ariella free. He pushed her backward, forcing her to sit on the couch, as he had initially instructed her to do.

"You're not a guest," Ariella spat.

He thrust his gun from its holster, pointing it at Ariella's forehead. "Are you sure about that?"

I couldn't let anything happen to my new friends. "Please, I'll go with you, just whatever you do, don't hurt them."

He yanked me by the hair and dragged me outside. I didn't fight back. How could I without risking my new friends' lives?

He pulled out a set of metal handcuffs. "Hands behind your back!" he barked.

I did as instructed, and he snapped on the cuffs nice and tight. It dug into my flesh, piercing my skin.

He thrust open the back door and pointed for me to climb inside the car. I hurried inside, and he shoved a black bag over my head, making it impossible to see where he took me. He slammed the door shut.

Another door slam.

Within seconds, the car roared to life. He hit the gas, tearing away from the house.

Where was he taking me?

Would I ever see my friends again? What about my home? I had nothing with me. My purse was abandoned on the floor in Ariella's house, and my cell phone trashed hours earlier.

I needed help, and I didn't have the slightest clue what he wanted with me.

"Why are you doing this?" I asked, my voice tentative and afraid.

"Shut up!"

CHAPTER TWENTY-SEVEN

LINCOLN

"What do you mean, she's been taken? Who the hell grabbed her?" I paced the length of Jaxson's home, a lovely house, but at the moment, it felt small and confining.

The police were on the scene, taking Ariella and Hazel's statements.

Jaxson called me the moment he found out what had happened, when Ariella called him in tears.

She'd been sobbing about an intruder and another man named Enzo, and the rest had been hard to decipher until she had calmed down.

"I don't know his name, but he works for her husband," Hazel said a little too calmly.

My poker face was not doing me justice. "She's married?"

Why hadn't Harper told me that she was married to another man?

"It's clear the guy's a real winner," I muttered under my breath.

"Now's not the time," Jaxson said. He shot me a look of cool off or walk out. I wasn't leaving the scene. I needed to know every detail, whatever it took to find her, alive.

Ariella took a long, slow breath. "She didn't seem to know the man's name, but they kept talking about Enzo, her husband. It was clear she recognized the man who took her. Harper explained to me that she'd gotten married under false pretenses. She was in Vegas, inebriated, and by the sounds of it, maybe they'd even drugged her. She was scared of him, Lincoln."

My hands balled into fists at my side. "Bastards," I muttered. I'd kill anyone who ever harmed a hair on Harper's head.

Maybe she wasn't mine, but I wanted to protect her.

No, I *needed* to protect her. She needed someone to look out for her. She'd probably never had that in her entire life.

"There's something else you should know," Ariella said. She fiddled with her hands. "Enzo was at the restaurant this afternoon. That's why Harper panicked, but he wasn't alone."

"Who was with him?" Jaxson asked before I could say a word. "The man who came to the house and took her?"

"No, Jayden Scott," Ariella said.

The room spun. My jaw clenched, and I stopped pacing. "I'll kill him."

Jaxson turned toward me, his arms folded across his chest. "Go take a walk."

I opened my mouth to respond, but he pointed toward the door. I knew he was right, trying to protect me. I couldn't make threats like that in front of the sheriff. What if the bastard winded up dead?

Good!

I stormed out of the house and slammed the door behind myself. The ground crunched under my feet as I stomped over the gravel toward my truck. The night air was cool but not frigid.

Why had one of Enzo's goons shown up and taken her?

Why did Jayden have lunch with Enzo? I climbed into my truck and started the engine.

The front door of the house opened, and Jaxson stepped out and stood on the porch.

"Where are you going?" he shouted.

I didn't answer him. He knew me well enough to know where I was headed.

I needed to speak to Jayden.

I tore down the mountain at lightning speed and headed for Jayden's newest place of employment. If I was lucky, he was working a shift. If I wasn't, then I didn't know where I'd find him.

His house had been demolished with the off-gridders during the attack about six weeks ago. The land had been abandoned, and I hadn't heard of anyone living up there again.

He was out there somewhere, getting into who the hell knows what trouble.

The road was dry, which made for plenty of traction as I hurried to the bar. I slammed on the brakes, shut off the engine, and jumped out of the truck, rushing inside.

My feet thudded against the floor, ready for a fight. Jayden barely so much as paid me any attention on my entrance.

"I'm just saying, I know how to move merchandise," Ben said as he sat at the bar, nursing a beer, speaking to Jayden.

I'd recognize that scumbag anywhere.

What the hell was Ben still doing in Breckenridge? Were the authorities out looking for him? Although at the moment, they were all tied up at Jaxson's house dealing with Harper's disappearance. Had he known that?

"Benjamin Ryan," I said with a gruffness as I headed straight for the two most wanted men of Breckenridge and not for their charm or charisma.

Ben dug out a wad of cash and dropped it on the counter. He shot one look at me, eyes wide, and darted out the back door.

Fuck.

Do I chase him down or deal with Jayden?

I couldn't be in two places at once, and the rest of the Eagle Tactical team was busy. Grabbing my phone, I texted Jaxson to give him a heads up.

If he wanted to come down and string up Ben by the balls, then, by all means, I wanted him to have the opportunity.

Sighing, my choice had already been made up. Maybe I should have gone after Ben, since he was still a threat to Ariella, but I needed to find Harper. She was the one in danger right this moment.

"We need to talk." I thundered around behind the bar, closing in on Jayden's personal space.

He wasn't the least bit smaller or less intimidating than I was, but he knew I'd kick his ass. We'd served together as brothers overseas.

Over the last few years, we'd become estranged. He'd been tied up in some dirty shit with the off-gridders that hadn't ended well for him.

"I don't have anything to say," Jayden quipped.

Maybe it was time for him to clean up and shape up.

"Are you sure about that?" I stared him down. "You were seen having lunch with a gentleman by the name of Enzo."

Jayden shrugged, not denying the truth. "So I was, since when is having a meal a crime?"

"Did you consort with Enzo and his goons in a plan to kidnap Harper Madison?" I grabbed Jayden by his shirt lapels, demanding an answer.

"What? No. I don't know anything about that," Jayden said, shrugging me off him.

I let go, only because I believed him. "Did you happen to know that Harper was allegedly married to Enzo?"

He stepped back, putting distance between us. "Is that supposed to mean something to me? I don't care who he marries or what he does with the women he desires," Jayden said.

"You ought to care, because she's been abducted and forced to do God knows what against her will."

Jayden grabbed a rag from the bar and began shining the wood surface. "Maybe it wasn't against her will. Perhaps she liked it, or maybe, better yet, she wanted to go with him."

I launched forward and pummeled him with my fist. "You bastard!" With my fist, I gripped him by the back of the head and slammed his face against the edge of the bar.

"Okay! Okay!" Jayden shouted, his nose bloody.

I let go, not intending to kill him, just force him to tell me the truth. He owed me that much after all I did for him when we served together.

"I don't know where she is or who took her," Jayden said.

I raised my fist, and he held up a hand to indicate that he wasn't done.

"Enzo bought some land around here, under a pseudo corporation. He's expanding his enterprise and planning on finishing what the off-gridders started some time ago."

"And what is that, exactly?"

Jayden's jaw was tight. A flash of something crossed his face.

Was it fear?

"Not for me to say, but he might take your girl there. It's pretty remote, makes the off-gridders home look like paradise."

Damn. "Do you have an address?"

"Can't say I do, but I'm sure with your Eagle Tactical expertise and connections, you can figure it out."

"Does Enzo have a last name?" I asked.

"Ricci. His name is Enzo Ricci, but you didn't hear it from me."

CHAPTER TWENTY-EIGHT

HARPER

I found it difficult to breathe.

My heart hammered against my chest as I sat in the backseat, my hands bound behind my back. I couldn't free myself from the metal that dug into my skin.

Pleading with my captor wouldn't help, either. I didn't even know his name. I tried forcing the memory to surface from that night in Vegas. I'd definitely seen him before, but it was all an intense blur.

Why did Enzo want me?

Was it because I was his wife? A stupid piece of paper and words spoken had bound us together, but it could all be undone. Right?

That is, if he didn't have other plans for me.

Why was Enzo in Breckenridge? Why hadn't he tracked me down in Los Angeles or elsewhere?

Was it because there was less security on location than on the studio set?

None of it made sense.

He opened the windows of the car, the breeze loud as it whirled around me, the dark cloth making it impossible to see or feel against my face.

The car jolted as we hit a bump in the road. I wasn't buckled in and tossed around the backseat.

The driver slammed on the brakes, not helping matters, landing my face against the headrest before falling back onto my butt.

"Stay here," he grunted. He shut off the car, and the front door squeaked open and shut.

Silence.

I recognized Enzo's voice from the restaurant. "Where the fuck have you been?" Enzo demanded. His voice carried through the open window.

"I brought you a present in the backseat," he said. "Want to take a look?"

"I don't like surprises, Zan."

Zan's rough laugh sent a shudder down my spine. "I wouldn't call it a surprise, boss. She's your wife."

"Fuck!"

I swallowed the lump in my throat. My mouth dry.

"You really know how to ruin an operation," Enzo said. "You disappoint me, Zan. Do you know what I expect of men who disappoint me?"

Zan cleared his throat. "Boss, I just wanted to show my appreciation. Please, don't do this."

Was he begging?

"Bringing her here could destroy everything I've worked to achieve. I cannot have loose ends." Enzo's voice carried louder, more insistent, etched with not just disappointment but anger. His voice grew louder.

"Please," Zan begged. "I promise I'll get rid of her. No one has to know it was me."

"You idiot! She's my wife. The first place they'll check is here. They're going to be looking for me!" His voice boomed and carried through the car.

I shivered and pulled my body smaller, tighter, wanting to be invisible.

"You've disgraced the family."

"Please, Enzo. I beg of you, I have a wife and two daughters," Zan said, his voice trembling.

"Then do yourself the honorable task, or I will make sure they suffer with you."

What honorable task?

What did Enzo want Zan to do?

Was that a threat?

"Forgive me, Enzo," Zan said.

Bang!

A shudder rippled through my body.

I became one with the seat, curled up, and bent down, as I shoved my body onto the floor. Hidden.

It became harder to breathe beneath the darkened hood that covered my face. Each breath expelled from my lungs took two gulps of air to replace.

I began hyperventilating.

Heavy boots stomped over the ground. The sound came closer. The door squeaked on its hinges as it was opened.

I stayed curled up on the floor in a ball, my head bent down with the thick black bag over my head.

He yanked the material from over my face. It took no time for my eyes to adjust. It remained dark outside. I stumbled backward, moving to the opposite end of the car, away from him.

"*Tesero*, you need to come with me," Enzo said.

I shook my head. My name wasn't *Tesero*. I didn't even know what that word meant. It sounded Italian, and I didn't speak a word of Italian.

Enzo held out his hand for me.

How could I take it, even if I wanted to? My arms were behind my back, my hands cuffed.

He grabbed me by the arm and dragged me out of the car.

"Turn around," he demanded. "Face the car." I did as I was told.

How far could I run? It was difficult to see much in the darkness of night. The moon was obstructed from view, the thick clouds overhead. There weren't any nearby houses or porches with their lights on, except for the one just a few yards away.

We were in the middle of nowhere.

How long had we driven? It hadn't been that far.

Were we still in Breckenridge?

"Did you kill Zan?" I asked. I'd caught his name while the two men had been arguing about me.

His hands were rough, his fingers thick and warm. He undid the handcuffs. Was I free to go?

Enzo spun me around, trapped between him and the side of the car.

"That is none of your concern," Enzo said. His eyes were dark. "Come with me." He grabbed my arm and yanked me to follow him.

I wanted to run.

Where would I go? I had no phone, didn't know where I was or how to get away. How far was the next property? Darkness stretched on as far as I could see.

We stepped away from the car and toward the house.

Zan lay in a pool of his own blood, the metal of a gun glistening beneath the stars in his hand. Had he shot himself or had Enzo made it look like that on purpose?

"Keep walking." Enzo's clasp on my arm remained tight as he escorted me up the porch steps and inside his extravagant home.

"What do you want with me?" I asked. From what I'd heard, Enzo hadn't been behind my abduction, but why keep me? What did he intend to do with me now that I was here on his property, taken by his men?

"Relax, *Tesero*. I will have a cup of tea for you, and you will be on your way." Enzo escorted me into his home and shut the door behind us.

I trembled as I inched forward, my legs not wanting to cooperate. Hell, I didn't want to cooperate. "Let me go. Please, I won't tell anyone you were involved."

Was that what he was worried about?

The floors were made of gray and white swirled marble. My bare feet were cold over the slick material as he dragged me into what I presumed to be his office. A tall chair sat in the corner, his desk the centerpiece. "Have a seat," he said, pushing me into the dark blue velvet seat.

I collapsed into the chair, grateful his touch was no longer on my arm. There were no windows in his office. The door was the only way to escape. The room was dark with no decoration, only wallpaper that glistened from the desk lamp that remained on.

"Sit. Stay."

"I'm not a dog," I said.

"I'll be right back. Just sit tight." Enzo walked backward several strides before he slipped out the door.

I leaped from the chair and hurried toward the door. He'd locked me inside. Why had I sat there and done as he'd commanded?

Why had I followed him inside his home? I should have run when I had the opportunity.

Without an obvious way to escape, I hurried toward his desk. The mahogany was in pristine condition, the wood clean and well maintained. There were no papers left askew. I tried the drawers. Each one had been locked.

The door swung open, and Enzo stalked inside, a silver tray with two cups of tea in hand as he stared at me. "I thought I told you to sit and wait for me?"

"I don't take orders from you or anyone else."

Enzo stepped closer toward me.

I took a step back, away from his desk, wanting to keep my distance.

What did he want with me?

"I've already contacted the authorities."

"What? You did?" I didn't believe him.

Why would he do that? There was a dead body in his front yard.

Was he going to blame me for that man's death?

"They will be here soon to ask you questions. I think it would be wise for you to sit and have a drink while we wait. We could talk, get the opportunity to know a little about one another," Enzo said.

I didn't trust him, but he wasn't waving a gun at me or threatening me, either. That was at least a good sign.

"You called the police?" I asked. "Why would you do that?"

"So, they can see that I'm innocent. I took no part in your abduction. I'm not a monster."

He offered me the tea, placing the tray on the desk. "But you killed that man on your front lawn."

Enzo eyed his watch, his jaw tight. He lifted a cup, the china small and delicate, which looked almost rather comical in his large rough hands. "I don't know about you, but I could use some chamomile to calm down." He lifted the teacup to his lips and took a sip.

"Chamomile?" That was my favorite, especially when my nerves were shot. I approached the desk, the thick wood keeping a distance between us, which made me feel safe.

I lifted the delicate material to my lips, having a sip.

"Yes, it's my favorite. I don't drink tea that often, but when I do, I always prefer a cup of chamomile," he said.

Maybe he wasn't all bad? I smiled wistfully into the cup and took another sip. "Yes, mine too."

"I am sorry, Harper," Enzo said, calling me by name. Had he mistaken my name for *Tesero,* or had he bequeathed a pet name on me?

Sighing, I sipped the tea, the liquid hot but not burning my mouth. I swallowed the dark liquid, my body beginning to relax. Already, I felt better, calmer.

The china slipped out of my hands and crashed onto the floor at my feet. I opened my mouth to apologize, but no sound came out. My legs grew weak, my arms didn't cooperate, and as my body began to collapse to the ground, Enzo caught me before I hit the floor.

"Sleep now, *Tesero*." He kissed my forehead.

Inside, I screamed. I shouted. I begged for him to let me go.

I was paralyzed, and he held me in his arms, before my vision went dark.

CHAPTER TWENTY-NINE

LINCOLN

"Lincoln," I answered my phone. Seeing as how it was Jaxson, I took the call outside the bar. I didn't need Jayden overhearing anything and calling Enzo. I didn't trust Jayden.

"I just got word from Sheriff Nelson. He received notification that Harper Madison is at Enzo Ricci's residence."

I held my breath. "Do you have an address?"

"Yes." He relayed the address to me, and I climbed into my truck and high-tailed it across town to the property that Enzo had recently purchased.

The sheriff had already arrived on the scene. Jaxson waited with news to find out what I needed from him. I didn't trust that she was there and this wasn't a setup.

In front of the house, was the blue Lotus that I'd seen earlier in the week. There were a few other vehicles along with the sheriff's car outside.

I pulled out my flashlight and walked along the darkened path up toward the house. A body lay covered with a sheet.

Shit.

Was it Harper?

No one had warned me that she might be dead.

Had Enzo called to confess? I hadn't asked. I should have, but I'd been too afraid to hear the answer.

I bent down and held my breath. I pulled back the edge of the sheet to reveal a man with thick dark hair and a gunshot wound to the head.

It wasn't Harper.

I exhaled a relieved sigh and covered the body back up with the sheet.

"Lincoln!" the sheriff shouted at me from the front porch. "Use gloves or don't touch that damned body."

Shit. I knew that. I hadn't touched the corpse, but I should have been thinking more about it being an active crime scene.

Was the dead man the person who had grabbed Harper and taken her against her will? How was he connected to Enzo?

I hurried up the porch steps toward Sheriff Nelson. "Have you seen Harper yet?"

"Yes, the news media will be here any minute, and we need to get her out of here and to the nearest hospital before people start snapping pictures and trample the crime scene."

Who called the press? Had they gotten wind of her abduction? Had the news media been listening to the police scanner and discovered that she'd been found?

"I'll take her." I wasn't leaving her side.

I rushed past the sheriff and stammered in through the front door. "Harper?" I shouted, listening for her sweet voice.

What had Sheriff Nelson meant about needing to get her to the hospital? It was a two-hour drive, and he hadn't mentioned the local clinic, so it had to be pretty bad. Was she injured? What had they done to her?

"Lincoln?" Her soft voice carried through the corridor.

"She's this way," said an Italian man with a fancy suit and thick dark hair. I didn't know if he was Enzo or someone else, but I followed.

Harper sat in a tall blue chair in a darkened office. Bookshelves lined the walls at every corner. There were no windows, just a desk lamp that illuminated the dimly lit room. The overhead lights appeared off or not working.

"Are you okay?" I asked, bending down to her level.

"What am I doing here?" Harper asked me. Her eyes were glazed and squinty, her lips dry. Had she been drugged? "Enzo?" Her brow furrowed as she glanced from me to the Italian man hovering beside me. "I don't remember anything."

"I'm going to take you to the hospital," I said. I lifted her with ease into my arms and carried her through the corridor and outside.

The sheriff opened my passenger door, and I gently placed Harper into my truck, letting her sit in the front seat beside me.

"I'm tired," Harper said. She struggled to keep her eyes open.

"What did they give you?" I doubted she knew the answer, and I wanted to run back inside Enzo's and pound the shit out of him, but my focus needed to be on Harper.

She was here, alive, and I needed to get her help.

Harper didn't answer me.

"Stay with me," I said, worried she might fall unconscious. I didn't know if she'd wake up, go into a coma, or something even worse.

I reached for the seatbelt and buckled her into the seat, making sure she was secure. "I'm going to take her over to the hospital to get bloodwork done," I said to the sheriff. "See if you can find out what they gave her."

"I'll call you if I find anything," Sheriff Nelson said.

I hurried to the driver's side, hopped in, and tore out for the hospital. It was a long drive. I dialed Jaxson while on my way.

"Hey, any news?" Jaxson asked.

"I have Harper with me in the front seat. She looks like they gave her some type of drug. She seems heavily sedated, can't move around, and doesn't remember what happened. She seemed surprised to see Enzo when I showed up."

"Was Enzo in handcuffs? Did he confess to her kidnapping?" Jaxson asked.

My grip tightened on the steering wheel. "No, there was a dead man outside his house. I'm guessing Enzo's blaming Harper's disappearance and abduction on him."

"Bastard," Jaxson muttered. "We'll meet you at the hospital."

"That isn't necessary," I said, glancing beside me at Harper as she mumbled incoherently under her breath. She didn't seem fully awake or alert. "I can call you as soon as we hear anything further."

"Please, do that," Jaxson said. "I'll let the other guys know what's going on."

I hung up the phone and hit the gas harder, hurrying to the hospital. "Hang on, Harper."

CHAPTER THIRTY

HARPER

Beep. Beep. Beep.

The sound of machines pulled me from my reverie.

My eyes lazily opened as bright whiteness cascaded all around me. My vision hadn't focused yet. I felt tired, drugged.

A strong, warm hand gripped mine.

I froze.

"Harper?" Lincoln's soothing voice reached my ears. "Harper, it's me, Lincoln."

I let my eyelids drift shut, a faint smile on my lips. I should have been angry with him but all I felt was a warmth sense of calmness come over me.

"I know," I mumbled.

I was safe.

My memories fuzzy and faded, I couldn't remember any of it. Everything felt hazy behind a cloud that my mind refused to lift.

"Sleep," Lincoln whispered.

I did just that, let my body succumb to sleep.

I didn't know how long I slept or how long Lincoln's hand remained latched in mine. Time seemed not to exist.

My head began to grow less foggy, and as I came to, Lincoln lay in a chair pulled up beside the bed, his hand in mine, his eyes closed. Asleep.

I didn't want to wake him.

What was I doing here? I had an IV in my left hand. My right hand, Lincoln had clasped and even in sleep hadn't let go of.

I wanted to go home. Crawl into my warm bed and sleep for a week. Except I was far away from Los Angeles.

Did I need to worry that my husband would come back for me? He was the one responsible for having me taken, wasn't he?

"Harper?" Lincoln mumbled, his eyelids opened, staring at me. "You're awake." He rubbed the sleep from his eyes and sat up straighter. "Let me get the nurse."

I held his hand, my grip tightening. I didn't trust hospitals or doctors. I didn't trust too many people, but Lincoln, while maybe I was supposed to be mad at him, the anger had melted away. He was with me here now when it mattered.

"Don't," I said. I didn't want him to leave my bedside. "Aren't you supposed to be my bodyguard?"

Lincoln's brow furrowed, and he grimaced.

Had I said something wrong?

He reached for the call button and pressed it. "They need to examine you," Lincoln said.

"Why am I here? What happened?" I asked.

"What do you remember?" He stayed at my bedside, his hand in mine.

The curtain rattled as a nurse pulled it open. "Ms. Madison, I see that you're awake. That's good news. Let me page the doctor." She hurried out of the room, leaving the two of us alone.

"I was over at Ariella's house with Hazel. We ordered a pizza, and this guy showed up, dragged me out and down to his car. He handcuffed me, blindfolded me, and took me for a ride. The rest, I don't remember. What happened, Lincoln?" My voice hitched as I trembled beneath the covers.

I shivered. The room was icy, and the smell of antiseptic only made me cringe. "Did Enzo do something to me? Why am I in the hospital?" I didn't feel sick or hurt. I couldn't remember the incident. Was that why I was hooked up to machines. How long had I been here?

"Enzo reported your appearance to the police," Lincoln said.

That didn't make sense. "What?" Why would he do that?

"He called the sheriff's office. You don't remember anything else after you were put into the car?"

I shook my head no. All of it was a blackout. "We were in the car. I was in the back seat and nothing after that."

"The sheriff found the man who took you dead, Zan Marino. It appears that he committed suicide. He was found outside of Ricci's home with a self-inflicted gunshot wound to the head. The lab is testing Enzo for gunshot residue, but we're pretty sure Enzo will be clean."

"Zan killed himself?" That made even less sense to me. "Why abduct me and then bring me to Enzo only to kill himself?"

Lincoln squeezed my hand. With his other one, he brushed a strand of hair out of my face and behind my ear. "I'm pretty sure Enzo wasn't behind your abduction, but I think he ordered Zan to kill himself, or he made it look like Zan committed suicide."

"Who would do something like that?" I mean, I knew it was Enzo, but I didn't understand why. His motivation, what would possess another man to follow?

"Enzo's part of the crime syndicate."

"The Italian Mob." I had surmised as much from the articles that I'd discovered recently about his business and his practices, which were shady. The government had nothing on him, but that didn't mean they weren't watching him. Hopefully, they'd find something and put him behind bars.

"You didn't tell me you were married," Lincoln whispered, his gaze staring into mine.

The doctor stepped into the room, my chart in his hands. "It's good to see that you're awake and alert, Heather."

I swallowed nervously as he used my legal name, my real name. No one called me by that, ever. Had they fished out my identification from my purse that I had left at Ariella's house?

He retrieved a penlight from his front pocket. "Follow the pen," the doctor instructed.

The doctor briefly examined me and then explained that the drugs were all out of my system and that I was free to leave. The bout of amnesia from the abduction may never return, but I shouldn't suffer any lasting effects from the drugs that had been forced into my body.

"The nurse will get the paperwork, and you're free to go," the doctor said. He headed out of the room, leaving Lincoln and me together.

Silence filled the small space. "I'll call a cab," I said. "You can head home." I didn't want to be a burden.

"It's a two-hour drive to Breckenridge, and there is likely to be press outside of your hotel. We'll be lucky if they're not outside the hospital when we leave," Lincoln said.

"Oh." Wonderful. Just what I wanted to deal with tonight.

"I'll take you back home. Well, to Breckenridge."

"Thanks," I said and sighed. I dropped his hand from mine. My fingers played over the white sheet, staring down at the cotton material.

Lincoln let the silence thicken like a cloud. The nurse eventually came back in, I signed the papers, got dressed with Lincoln waiting out in the hallway, and then he helped me down to his truck.

We had barely spoken two words since I was discharged.

Tension sizzled in the air between us like lightning, ready to strike.

"Here we are." Lincoln unlocked the truck, and I climbed inside, buckling myself. It was well past midnight.

"Are you sure you're okay to drive back tonight? Maybe we should get a hotel room?" I suggested. I didn't have anything to change into, but at least he wouldn't fall asleep behind the wheel.

Lincoln shut my door and stalked around to the driver's side. He climbed into the truck. "I'd rather sleep in my own bed tonight."

He started the truck.

"Okay."

More silence filled the vehicle as he pulled out of the hospital parking lot and drove us toward Breckenridge.

I stared out the side window. I should have been tired, but I wasn't. I felt more awake than I'd been in quite a long time.

Maybe it was the adrenaline, or perhaps something else? What had I been drugged with? Who had drugged me, Enzo or Zan? Did it matter?

I hated the silence.

It made me feel even more uncomfortable. I glanced at Lincoln as he stared at the road, both hands tight on the steering wheel. Was he mad at me?

"Are we going to talk about the fact you're married?" Lincoln asked. "Or that your husband runs the Italian Mafia?"

I licked my lips. "You know that saying what happens in Vegas stays in Vegas, well, getting married doesn't stay in Vegas."

"Is that supposed to be funny?" Lincoln shot.

I shrugged. "I guess not. I met him in Vegas. We danced together, got drunk, and somehow ended up at a wedding chapel marrying each other. I don't really remember much of it, just that I woke up with a really bad hangover the next day, and I had a diamond on my ring finger. I snuck out, vowed to forget about it, and move on. I didn't even know his name that morning."

"They let you marry him while you were intoxicated?" Lincoln fumed. "Didn't you need a marriage license that you get at a courthouse before going to the chapel?"

I gave a shrug. "Yes, but one of his buddies worked at the courthouse. He acted like he was doing us a favor."

"Maybe doing Enzo a favor. He certainly wasn't doing you one." Lincoln's grip tightened on the steering wheel.

I didn't want to be married to Enzo. Didn't Lincoln see that? "I called a lawyer to find out if the marriage was legally binding and because I was intoxicated at the time of the marriage, I can get the marriage annulled if Enzo is willing to, on the grounds that I wasn't capable of consenting or understanding what I was doing. If not, then we have to legally obtain a divorce. I hadn't spoken to him since Vegas. I didn't even know his name until a copy of the marriage certificate was sent to me."

"I'll get you that divorce if that's what you want," Lincoln said.

"It honestly is." I wanted nothing to do with Enzo, now or in the future. All ties between us, I wanted severed. "I'm sorry that I didn't tell you. It's not something I talk about, ever."

CHAPTER THIRTY-ONE

ARIELLA

Curled up in Jaxson's arms, in his bed, I'd found it difficult to sleep.

"You're still awake?" Jaxson whispered, his eyes open, the light from the nearby clock offering a hint of light in the darkened bedroom.

"Yes," I said and sighed. How was I going to sleep after today's events? Thankfully, Harper had been found, but I didn't feel better about her being taken and dragged away by a mafia thug.

Small towns were supposed to be safe.

Jaxson reached for his phone, glancing at the screen briefly. "Lincoln texted that they're on the way back from the hospital."

I exhaled a heavy sigh of relief. "She's okay?"

"I think so," Jaxson said.

Silence filled the room. His warm grip held me again at my waist, cuddling me to him. He smelled wonderful, and my body relaxed against him, but my mind wouldn't slow down.

"Hazel knows about us," I said.

"That's not a surprise. Lincoln saw us making out at the hospital," Jaxson reminded me.

"You're okay with people knowing about us?" Why were we continuing to hide our relationship? Little by little, our friends and colleagues had discovered what we'd been doing, sneaking around together.

We were two grown adults. Happy adults. Why did we have to hide it any longer?

He pulled me tighter, rolling us around so that I was on top. His hands slid under my pajama shirt, and he began rubbing my back in soft, soothing motions.

"I think by now everyone knows," Jaxson muttered with a laugh. "Hiding of it seems kind of pointless."

I rolled us around again, bringing him to lie above me, pinning me down. I liked when he was on top and took command, especially in the bedroom. I let my fingers dance along the rim of his boxers.

"What about Skylar and Izzie?" I asked, holding him tight against me. I didn't want him to pull away.

"Skylar is a grown woman. She's heard us having sex," Jaxson said with a laugh. "Seems silly to continue to hide it from her. Besides, she's hardly ever around. I like to be cautious around Izzie, but we're not friends with benefits. I love you."

"I love you too," I whispered. "Honestly, I've been worried. I know you wanted me to call that therapist, but I just can't do it. I hate opening up to strangers. It's hard enough for me to talk with you about my feelings. I keep worrying that they'll tell me to move out. That living with my boss and hiding our relationship is unhealthy."

"What?" Jaxson's brow furrowed. "I don't want you to leave, Ariella. If I haven't made that perfectly clear, this is your home, with Izzie and me. I hope we haven't made you feel unwelcome."

"Gosh, no. You've been wonderful. It's just sleeping in a different room, hiding our relationship. It makes me feel dirty."

"I never want you to feel that way, ever. From now on, you sleep with me in here," Jaxson said. "I like having you in my bed, knowing that you're safe."

"I like that too."

CHAPTER THIRTY-TWO

LINCOLN

I hadn't taken Harper back to her hotel room after the hospital. I didn't want to leave her alone.

She was right, I was her bodyguard, and she was my responsibility. I had taken her back to my place, let her crash on my bed, and I had contemplated the sofa, which would have been too small, when she let me join her.

I checked my phone early the following day. Jaxson had texted that the studio canceled the film shoot. I didn't know what that meant for Harper's career or if she'd be pissed or pleased by the news.

"Morning," she whispered. Her eyelids fluttered open as she lay on her side, staring at me.

"No work today, for either of us. It looks like the studio has put a hold on the production." Although there were a few things I wanted to do, I didn't have to run security detail on the set, which was a bonus considering what time we'd gotten into my place last night.

Harper rolled onto her back, staring up at the ceiling. "Good. I shouldn't have taken on the role, knowing I had to work for that asshat of a director."

"Well, if you hadn't, we never would have met." I doubted that she'd have found her way to Breckenridge on her own.

"True."

I rubbed the sleep from my eyes and climbed out of bed. "The workers will be here soon to work on the restaurant downstairs." There would be no chance of sleep with all the banging going on.

"What happened to your restaurant? Piss off someone? Are those real bullet holes?" Harper asked.

"Unfortunately, they are as real as they come. I did want to stop by Eagle Tactical this afternoon and find out if there's any word on Enzo and if he's being charged with murder or your abduction."

Harper remained quiet. Should I not have brought it up?

She sat up in bed, the blankets at her waist, her clothes from yesterday still on. "I should go back to the hotel, shower, and change."

"I'll drive you. Do you mind if I hop in the shower real fast?"

"Only if I can join you," she whispered.

I leaned in, capturing her lips with mine, wanting her to know that, yes, I wanted her. I hadn't stopped wanting her since we'd laid eyes on each other. I grabbed her hand and pulled her to her feet, leading her to the bathroom.

I flipped on the light and started the shower. I quickly undressed and discarded my clothes, leaving them on the floor.

Harper hesitated, but her eyes raked over my body, taking all of it in. She chewed on her bottom lip.

Did she like what she saw? Was she unable to stop staring at me? It felt good to be wanted. I needed to make her feel the way that she made me feel inside.

"Do you want a hand?" I offered and closed the distance between us, my hands on her hips. My fingers skimmed her sides and stomach as I inched the material up.

Harper lifted her arms into the air. I gently guided her shirt up and over. My fingers pinched the bra band, undoing the clasp in the back, letting the straps slide down her shoulders and flow to the floor.

Her lips looked warm and inviting. I leaned in, kissing her, tasting her, while my fingers went to work at her pants, pushing her slacks down along with her panties.

Wrapping my arms around her, I dragged her into the shower, under the spray, our bodies together, the heat caressing our skin.

Her hands explored my back and down to my ass. She gave it a firm slap.

I quirked an eyebrow, staring down at her. "Did you just spank me?"

She laughed and nodded, giving a wide grin as she did it again.

I grabbed her wrist and pinned her against the shower tile. Her nipples hardened, and my mouth fell hard onto hers as I slipped a hand between us, touching her.

She moaned and gasped in pleasure as I separated her folds, feeling over her wetness. I teased her pearl, her body shuddered, and her breathing only further intensified.

Her hand reached down between us, teasing my length, playing with the head, making my hips thrust. Oh God, she was killing me.

Closing the gap between us, I teased her entrance, the heat of the shower steaming up the bathroom. The room felt warm, sweltering, but I didn't care. Her cheeks were flushed, and a blush spread across her chest.

Swiftly, I entered her, driving deeper, harder, listening to her soft pleas in my ear.

"More." She wrapped her legs around me, pulling me closer.

I did as she instructed, burying myself inside her, every inch, until she and I were one.

Harper's head tipped back, and her moans grew louder and more insistent with need. I held her tight against me. One hand snaked between us to bring her over the edge.

She sounded close.

Harper tightened with each thrust.

She felt close.

I struggled to hang on.

"Please," Harper gasped, her eyes slamming shut, and her fingernails clinging to my shoulder, marking me. I was hers.

I withdrew, listening to her whimper in protest. I shut off the shower. So much for getting clean.

"Why did you stop?" Her breathing was raspy. She'd been on the edge, and I withdrew, teasing her.

"Because you deserve more than a shower fuck," I whispered into her ear, nibbling her skin.

She purred under my touch. I carried her out of the shower, back to the bed.

"I swear if you don't let me finish, I may just have to tie you up to the bedposts and have my way with you," Harper said.

A smirk crossed my lips. "Is that so? That doesn't sound bad at all." I guided her down to the mattress. My body hovered above hers, teasing her entrance.

"You're a fucking tease," Harper moaned. She grabbed my girth and forced me to lose all coherent thought as I entered her.

A huge smile etched across her face, pleased with her work.

Each thrust grew deeper, more intense and fulfilling, as I drew near.

I didn't want this moment to end. If the film shoot was done, then was Harper leaving?

I wanted to convince her to stay here for me.

My fingers slipped down, teasing her pearl. Her hands clutched the bedsheets, and her back arched off the mattress.

Her moans intensified, each more pronounced and sexier than the last. She gasped for air, her insides tightening on me, bringing me toward oblivion with her.

She shuddered and let go, panting hard, struggling to catch her breath.

I understood completely.

Several more thrusts, and I was there with her, drowning inside her warmth, breathing with her as one.

My heart pounded, and it was the only sound mixed with our breathing that filled my ears. Slowly, I withdrew and rolled onto my back.

Hot and sweaty, I could use another shower.

CHAPTER THIRTY-THREE

HARPER

I packed my bags at the motel. The rental car awaited me outside. It was time to return to Los Angeles.

There was a sharp, resounding knock on the door.

"Just a sec!" I shouted. I zipped my bag and hurried to the door, glancing out the peephole before seeing Lincoln on the other side.

"Hey," he said, greeting me with a sly grin.

I couldn't hide the smile on my face, either. Earlier that morning, we'd spent a good half hour in the shower, not the very least bit bathing and then quite a while tangled in the sheets. I could have spent forever in bed with the man, but that wasn't a realistic possibility.

I had to return home. The film shoot was canceled. The director had resigned, and after the public news of my kidnapping, the studio put a firm hold on the production indefinitely.

At least the studio wasn't blaming me, but they felt I needed time to recover.

"Did you come to say goodbye?" I asked.

In his hands, he held a manila folder. "While you came back to the hotel to pack, I took it upon myself to have a word or two with Enzo."

My stomach somersaulted. "You did." What did that mean?

He stepped inside my hotel room and approached the desk. "Enzo will be out of your life forever. All you have to do is sign the papers." He pulled out the pages and laid them on the table for me to see.

"What are these?" I hesitated before I stepped forward, needing to read the contents. It was as thick as a book.

"Divorce papers. You and Enzo can go your separate ways."

What was he up to? I scoured the papers, reading as fast as I possibly could. "Enzo agreed to this?" I asked.

I stared at the pages. I was no lawyer, but it looked solid and acceptable for both parties. I would get none of Enzo's assets, and he would get none of mine. I would accept those terms. I didn't marry him for whatever wealth he had accumulated, and I sure as hell wasn't giving up anything of mine to him.

Flipping through page after page, it was long but appeared agreeable.

"How did you do this?" I asked as I lifted the pen from the desk and scribbled my signature.

"I had a few words with Enzo this morning. He already had the papers drawn up. It was as much his idea as mine."

That surprised me. "Do we need a witness?"

"No, but you will have to go before the county judge. As soon as you're ready, you can do so in any county or state together."

I groaned. The thought of seeing Enzo again made me want to vomit.

"I'll be with you the entire time," Lincoln said. "Ariella and Hazel offered to come too. They want to throw you a divorce party."

"Okay, but we're not ordering pizza. The last time we did that, Zan showed up." While I realized there was no relation between the pizza delivery service and the mafia arriving at the door, it still was an association that I wasn't ready to get past.

"So, you'll stay a little longer?" Lincoln asked, his eyes filled with hope. "A few more days?" Did he want me to stay indefinitely?

"Yes, I can do that, a few more days. You know, if you're really that upset about me leaving, you could come with me to Los Angeles."

Lincoln smiled, tightlipped. "Los Angeles is so—"

"Sunny?"

"I was going to say smoggy. Don't you love the outdoors? The quiet and beauty of nature. You can't go rafting down the river with a view like we have in Los Angeles."

Was he trying to convince me to stay? It wasn't that hard. I did love it up here. The thought of going home wasn't really making me that happy.

"No, I guess you can't," I said, glancing at my bag on the bed. "But the beaches, you have to admit that is a perk, even with the smog."

He laughed under his breath. "Maybe I should be more direct. Stay for me," Lincoln said, pulling me into his embrace.

I wrapped my arms around his neck and tilted my face up, my lips caressing his. "Won't you get tired of me?"

"I don't believe that's possible." He didn't so much as loosen his hold on me, his arms wrapped around my lower back.

"Are you asking me to move in with you?"

A huge smile spread across Lincoln's face. "I swear if you're teasing me, woman, I don't think I can take it."

My lips crushed his. "Do you see me laughing?" I would need to return to Los Angeles, if only to bring back some of my things.

EPILOGUE

JAXSON

Life felt almost too good. I waited for the ball to drop. Harper was safe and home from the hospital. Mason had been released from medical care and was back to his old self.

Ben was out there, somewhere, waiting to strike. It wasn't over. Would it ever be?

We'd yet to run into him again, but we would. It was only a matter of time.

The Eagle Tactical team was over, along with their girlfriends, for a cookout. We vowed to spend more time together having fun. We deserved it.

I sat on the back porch at my house, the view of the mountains always a beauty.

Izzie chased butterflies down on the grass by the garden where Ariella and Harper were busy planting flowers.

Harper rested a hand on her very pregnant belly. She and Lincoln were expecting their first child, and Izzie was probably as excited as they were, looking forward to a new playmate.

Bear plopped down next to me on the wooden deck, her tail wagging, bathing in the afternoon sun.

"Look at this," Hazel said, showing me her social media account. There were dozens of photos, but she scrolled to one in particular. "Skylar's got a boyfriend."

"Oh yeah? Let me see."

I'd barely seen Skylar. She'd been working long hours and out partying most nights.

Hazel handed me her phone. I nearly dropped the device when the picture staring back at me ripped my insides to pieces. Jayden had his arm around Skylar, a huge grin on both of their faces.

I clicked on Skylar's account, scrolled through a few photos until I landed on one that made my stomach drop to the floor. She held up her left hand, revealing a flashy diamond on her ring finger.

"When the hell did she get engaged?"

————

Thank you for reading Conceal: Lincoln. Continue the adventure in the final book of the Eagle Tactical series with COVERT: JAYDEN!

Jayden wasn't the bad guy, just the bad boy, and I fell for him, hard.

Jayden

My niece has been missing for months and I've spent every waking hour tracking her down. I need a partner in crime, a woman on the inside who can help me gather intelligence.

Skylar is cute, snarky, and Jaxson's younger sister. She's completely off-limits and when my former military brother discovers that I've hired her in secret, he's going to kill me.

Skylar

Desperate for cash, I agree to an undercover operation with Jayden Scott. For two grand a week, I have to be his fake fiancée. There's more to the job; he wants me to sneak around inside his boss' house and find everything I can on his niece's whereabouts.

The plan goes south fast and I'm given an ultimatum: kidnap three girls by midnight or be sold at auction.

One-click COVERT: JAYDEN now!

And sign up for my newsletter to find out about new books, giveaways, and freebies: www. authorwillowfox.com/subscribe

I appreciate your help in spreading the word, including telling a friend. Reviews help readers find books! Please leave a review on your favorite book site.

GIVEAWAYS, FREE BOOKS, AND MORE GOODIES

I hope you enjoyed CONCEAL and will continue the journey with Jaxson, Ariella, and the Eagle Tactical team.

While this is my first series as Willow Fox, I've been published professionally since 2013.

Sign up for my Willow Fox newsletter

If you enjoyed CONCEAL, please take a moment to leave a review. Reviews helps other readers discover my books.

Not sure what to write? That's okay. It doesn't have to be long. You can share how you discovered my book; was it a recommendation by a friend or a book club?

Let readers know who your favorite character is or what you'd like to see happen next. Do you normally read HEA? How are you feeling about the HFN? (I hope satisfied but I promise I will be delivering a HEA at the end of the series!)

Thank you for reading! I hope you'll consider joining my mailing list for free books, promotions, giveaways, and new release news.

ABOUT THE AUTHOR

Willow Fox has loved writing since she was in high school (many ages ago). Her small town romances are reflective of living in a small town in rural America.

Whether she's writing romance or sitting outside by the bonfire reading a good book, Willow loves the magic of the written word.

She dreams of being swept off her feet and hopes to do that to her readers!

Visit her website at:

https://authorwillowfox.com

Eagle Tactical Series

Expose: Jaxson

Stealth: Mason

Conceal: Lincoln

Covert: Jayden

Mafia Marriages

Secret Vow

Captive Vow

Savage Vow

Unwilling Vow

Ruthless Vow

Bratva Brothers

Brutal Boss

Wicked Boss

Possessive Boss

Obsessive Boss

Boxsets

Eagle Tactical Collection

Looking for kinkier books? Try these spicy stories written
under the name Allison West.

Boxsets

Academy of Littles

Western Daddies Collection

Obey Daddy Collection

The Alpha Collection

Western Daddies

Her Billionaire Daddy

Her Cowboy Daddy

Her Outlaw Daddy

Her Forbidden Daddy

Standalone Romances

The Victorian Shift

Jailed Little Jade

Prefer a sweeter romance with action and adventure?
Check out these titles under the name Ruth Silver.

Aberrant Series

Love Forbidden

Secrets Forbidden

Magic Forbidden

Escape Forbidden

Refuge Forbidden

Boxsets

Gem Apocalypse

Nightblood

Royal Reaper

Royal Deception

Standalones

Stolen Art